For Auntie Rene – thanks for all the sewing lessons!

"I get by with a little help from my friends"

\- The Beatles

Chapter 1

"Are you ok down here Gran?"

It was half ten and even though I was emotionally exhausted, I couldn't make myself fall asleep so I'd come downstairs to make a cup of tea, just for something to do more than anything else.

Gran looked up from the book resting across her lap. "Oh Jess. Yes, I'm fine. I didn't seem to want to drift off"

"I know the feeling. Do you want a cuppa?"

"Go on then"

I flicked the light on in the kitchen and started to make the tea. I'd learned from an early age how Gran took her tea - strong with only a splash of milk. She said during the war, she'd gotten used to the shortage of sugar because of Rationing and never really acquired a taste for it again when it was back in good supply.

As the kettle boiled, I looked around the kitchen. On the surface, it all appeared the same. Everything was in its rightful place, always where it had been, but at the same time it all seemed so different. The whole house felt different. It was strange to think I would never again hear Grandad singing to himself when he was cooking or see him wear that silly sun hat he always wore when he was gardening.

The funeral had been lovely. Well, as lovely as funerals could be anyway. Gran had said she wanted it to be a celebration of his life rather than mourning his passing. She said if he looked down and saw us all miserable, listening to some dreary, generic bible passage being spouted out, he would never forgive us. Instead, old colleagues from the garage where he worked for over fifty years told hilarious stories about him. Gran had made sure all his favourite songs were played and the packed church sung along to the more upbeat ones. People had also been forbidden from wearing black because Grandad wouldn't have liked that either. He liked colour, the brighter the better, which was why his beloved garden was always an explosion of colour when it was in full bloom.

But tears were still shed.

The first time I had ever seen my father cry was when we had all gathered at the hospital after being told Grandad didn't have long left. It scared me slightly because I had never seen him so upset. During the funeral, I became worried. Dad seemed to be taking it very hard. He was usually so together, the rock of our family, but now he seemed to have lost all his strength. Gran, on the other hand, had been the most together out of all of us.

I carried the tea through and settled it down on the coffee table before perching myself on the arm of Gran's chair.

"What are you looking at?" I asked, peering down at the photo album she had resting across her knees. "Is that you?"

She nodded and gave a little smile that said *it was a wonderful time but I can't tell you everything about it because it would be a little inappropriate to think of your grandmother like that.*

I glanced down at the young woman in the black and white photo who beamed back at me. As I'd gotten older, I was regularly told how I was the spit of my grandmother in her youth. It was quite the compliment but she was definitely much prettier than I would ever be. I had inherited her light blue eyes, dark blonde hair and heart-shaped face. We were also a similar size and build - five foot nine and naturally slim. But in all the photos I had seen of her, she had worked it well, looking like a model where I was self-conscious of the thin figure and height that had always made me a bit gawky. I had never inherited her natural grace.

"How old were you then?"

"I was twenty-one. It was 1953, so not long after I'd met your grandfather."

I looked at the next photo and pointed at it. "And is that the legendary car?"

She let out her tinkly laugh. "The very same."

When I was a child, I'd asked Grandad to tell me the tale of how he and Gran met as a bedtime story. She'd been on her way into town to visit the new haberdashery. She was driving her father's old car, a 1948 Morris Six MS, which he'd recently given to her as a birthday present and she was going to buy some new fabric with her birthday money. Just before she made it into town, she noticed smoke coming from under the bonnet and the car started to judder. She pulled over and opened the bonnet, releasing a massive cloud of smoke which was spotted by a handsome young mechanic who just happened to be passing on his bicycle on his way to work. Being the gentleman he was, he stopped to help her and immediately thought she was the most beautiful girl he had ever seen and decided then and there that he would marry her. He patched the car up as best he could and managed to get it to the garage where he worked as a mechanic. He spent the rest of the morning fixing her car and when it was done, refused payment for it. Instead, he asked if he could take her out later that evening to the pictures. She accepted, he took her to see Roman Holiday and the rest became history.

It instantly became my favourite story. Much better than any fairy-tale from a book could ever be because it was real life.

"How are you really Gran? You've been so composed throughout this whole thing, making sure everyone else is ok, but how are you?"

She let out a sigh and smoothed down the long plait of white hair that ran over her left shoulder. She had always refused to have her hair cut into the traditional short length women were expected have when they reached a certain age. "It's been difficult. I'm not quite sure how I'm going to cope without him. But at the same time, if I get upset, I hear his voice in my head telling me not to be so silly and I should be enjoying my life while I still can."

Tears welled up in my eyes and I sniffed, which focused Gran's attention back onto me. She raised her hand and rested it on my cheek. "Oh my darling, don't cry. Yes, it's sad that he's not with us anymore but we still have all the wonderful memories that will keep him alive for us."

She was right and there were some truly wonderful memories. During the summer holidays, I had been allowed to stay with my grandparents for a whole four weeks at a time. Dad had moved away from his hometown when he was younger because of work, so we were a couple of hours away from Gran and Grandad. It was so nice to spend a long stretch of time with them and they always kept me busy. Grandad would take me fishing with him or let me help in the garden, teaching me the names of flowers and helping me to collect the ladybirds in a jar, so we could release them a later on and see them all fly off at once. There were also the numerous trips to the seaside or picturesque places in the countryside for picnics.

She took my hand in hers. "Anyway Jess, this is the first time I've seen you in a couple of months, how are things? You can't always tell me properly over the phone so tell me everything now."

If I were being completely honest, things were pretty shit.

I was living in London because Liam, my boyfriend, had been offered a wonderful job there. I'd left my job back home at a company that helped set up new businesses to go with him because he'd asked me to. Naively, I thought with my Business degree, I would have no trouble getting a job in London. We'd been there over a year and I still hadn't found anything. Liam was riding high in the world of insurance while I was living off temp-work, doing basic admin tasks. No one seemed to want to take me on full time. And to top it all off, I'd found out a week ago that Liam had been cheating on me with someone from his work, for at least the last couple of months. If it wasn't so sad, I'd laugh at how clichéd it all was.

"Things are good. London definitely keeps me busy." I replied brightly, lying through my teeth.

"Jessica Mary Crawford." There was that steely note of authority in Gran's voice that she very rarely used. "You were a terrible liar when you were seven and you're not much better at twenty-seven. Now tell me the truth."

I didn't want to tell her the truth because the focus this week had been on Grandad's death. No one needed to worry about how my life was going nowhere and my boyfriend was cheating on me with a woman with over the top fake breasts. But she wasn't going to relent and eventually I gave in, telling her everything. By the end of it I was in tears and I felt so selfish for being upset about this when we'd buried my grandfather earlier today. But this was the first time I'd admitted out loud how bad things were and I could no longer pretend that everything was fine.

Gran gave my hand a tight squeeze, which somehow made me feel a bit better. Or maybe it was just being around Gran. No matter what the problem, she had had a way of making you feel like everything was going to be ok.

"Oh Jess, I'm sorry. But you go ahead and have a good cry while we work out what you're going to do. First off, you need to leave that awful boyfriend of yours. I take it he doesn't know that you know about his indiscretions?"

I shook my head. "No. I'd had suspicions for a while but I just thought I was being paranoid. It was only by accident and good timing that I happened to see them coming out of a restaurant together when he was supposed to be having a lunch meeting. Oh Gran, he was all over her, it was horrible."

"If that had been me, I would have marched straight over to him and given him what for and left him with the bruises to enforce my point."

She probably would have as well.

"I was in such a state of shock that I didn't know what to do. I did the unspeakable thing of checking his phone when he left it on the worktop to go have a shower. Turns out it wasn't a one-off. It had been going on for a little while."

"Jess, you need to get out. You head straight back to London, give him a piece of your mind, get your things and get out."

"But I don't have anywhere to go." That was the saddest thing about it. "I'm not in permanent work, I have no savings because of it and as pathetic as it sounds, I don't really have any proper friends in London."

It really was pathetic, but it was the truth. Because I was essentially an office drifter, I was never around long enough to form proper friendships and I hated all of Liam's insurance friends and their partners.

"No granddaughter of mine is staying with a cheating arsehole because of some flimsy excuse like that. You obviously don't like London anyway so you need to leave. You can come and live with me - the change of scenery will do you the world of good."

"Oh Gran, I can't be a burden like that, I-."

"Don't argue with me Jessica. I've made up my mind. You can come and live here, rent free of course, and find yourself a job you love." Her voice broke ever so slightly. "And you'll be helping me too. Without your grandad here, I'm going to be terribly lonely in this house by myself and to be perfectly honest, I could do with the company. Who better than my favourite grandchild?"

I smiled in spite of myself. "I'm your only grandchild. But when you put it like that, I'd be an idiot not to take up your offer. Seriously Gran, thank you so much for this, you have no idea what it means to me."

"My darling, you don't need to thank me, it's what I'm here for. Now I think I might finally be ready for bed. We'll sort everything out in the morning and get you down to London to get your things as soon as possible. Honestly, what is wrong with men these days? If your grandfather were here, he would be down there himself kicking some sense into that boy."

I chuckled and kissed Gran on the cheek before emptying out the untouched tea in the sink and heading up to bed by myself. I was feeling better than I had in the last week. It was definitely going to be a different scene to London, but I thought I had more chance of finding my place in the small town of Pickney than I did in the Big City.

The following morning, I woke up with a new resolve and a fresh fighting spirit. Liam had made a fool out of me for long enough and I wasn't going to let him do it anymore.

Downstairs Gran was already dishing up breakfast for my parents. I noticed how Dad still didn't seem his usual self, Grandad's death having not quite sunken in yet.

"Morning love, did you sleep ok?" Mum asked as I entered the kitchen and started to make tea.

"Not too bad actually. Does anyone else want a cup?"

They all shook their heads as Gran immediately came up to me, brandishing an empty plate. "I think we're still drinking the last one. Now what can I fix you for breakfast? Once that's sorted, we can tell your parents the good news."

"Good news?" Dad looked up from the spot on the table he had been intently staring at.

"Yes. But let the poor girl get settled first Michael. Jess, what would you like to eat?"

"I'll just make myself some toast thanks."

After my toast had popped, I sat at the table with my breakfast and my parents were staring at me, waiting for me to talk.

"So this news. Well, erm, Gran has been nice enough to offer to let me come and live with her for a bit while I sort a few things out."

"But Jess, what about London? What about Liam?"

I twirled my hair around my finger nervously. My parents really didn't need to hear the whole story, so I attempted to give them only the essential details. "We're not together anymore. It's a pretty recent decision but I was planning to go round there this afternoon to get my things. And London hasn't been working out - I can't keep living off temp work. I definitely won't be able to live there by myself without full time work and I don't want to move in a house share with strangers. This at least gives me a chance to start afresh and start a real career again."

"I think it's a really good idea." Everyone's head turned to look at Dad, not expecting him to be the one to speak up. "Jess, I've been a bit worried about you while you've been in London and not just because of the non-permanent working situation. And Mum, I was going to worry about you being in this house all by yourself, but if Jess is going to be here, it will put my mind at rest on both counts. You can keep an eye on each other."

Gran was beaming at him. "I'm glad you approve Michael. I do think it is the right decision, don't you agree Julie?"

Mum hesitated for a moment but seemed to realise it was actually a plan that worked out for everyone. Plus, she was outnumbered. "I suppose so. As long as you're happy Jess. It's a shame though, I did like Liam."

She liked the old Liam she knew back in Stratford when he was polite, caring and considerate. She didn't know the current Liam who had been changed by the bright lights of London, who flaunted his large pay packet and cheated on his girlfriend. Current Liam was a complete tosser.

Now that Mum and especially Dad supported this decision, it only confirmed to me that I was making the right move here. It seemed to perk Dad up and I even caught him smiling occasionally. The familiar crinkle around his eyes was nice to see. Over lunch, he reminisced about the fishing trip with Grandad where he slipped and fell in the water while trying to wrestle a monster of a trout.

By late afternoon we finally said our goodbyes. I let out a sigh once their car had disappeared down the road of neat, uniformed houses. "I suppose it's time for me to go now as well."

"Are you sure you don't want me to come with you?"

"Positive, but thanks for the offer. I've got it all planned out in my head, so hopefully it will work out how I want it to. If it does, I should be home by about half seven."

"Call me if you need anything." She gave my shoulder a reassuring squeeze and handed me the keys to Grandad's old estate. I'd already put some boxes and bin liners on the back seat for a quick getaway.

As it was a Thursday, I was expecting Liam to be home about six. At least, that was as long as he didn't decide to spend a stolen hour with his bit-on-the-side and come back later than usual, claiming he had to work late.

The drive from Pickney to London usually took just over an hour, so I should arrive at our flat about half four, just before rush hour started to take effect. Now I thought about it, it was probably classed as Liam's flat and I was essentially his tenant. He'd picked it out and the lease was in his name alone. He paid the majority of the rent and bills, only accepting my contribution depending on how my own work was going. I wondered if this had been part of a long-term plan for him. If I didn't contribute anything to the flat and we did split up, I wouldn't have any claim to anything. At the end of the day, I was just a name on the Council Tax bill.

I pulled up outside the white building in Hammersmith and affixed my parking permit to the Volvo, the first time I had ever needed to use it. I carried the boxes and bin bags through and surveyed the flat before getting to work. It didn't take half as long as I expected because once I started pack things away, I realised the majority of it was Liam's anyway. Turns out my belongings filled up two of the boxes and one bin bag. I was sure I had more clothes than were hanging in my side of the wardrobe, but apparently I didn't. And they were all black and grey. I really needed to sort a new wardrobe out. I had some bits of jewellery Liam had bought me over the three years we were together, but I left these on the dresser not wanting to take anything that made me think of him. I dumped my boxes and bag in the back of the car and waited for Liam to come home.

The door opened at quarter to six, which surprised me but I was determined to keep my cool and leave with as much dignity as possible.

"Hey babe. I didn't think you'd be back. Did the funeral go ok? I meant to text you, but you know, work and all that."

I was leaning against the worktop staring at this man I didn't know. He was so different from the Liam I first fell in love with. This man with his cocky attitude, slicked-back blonde hair and hand-cut suits was not my Liam anymore. I missed my scruffy Liam from Stratford who always wore Converse and who liked to play the antique Pac-Man machine in our local pub.

He leaned in to kiss me but I turned my head and he caught my cheek instead of my lips. A whiff of perfume that wasn't mine immediately filled my nostrils.

"I just came to say goodbye." I said, surprised at how steady my voice was.

"Are you going out somewhere nice tonight?" He was already rummaging around in the fridge and pulled out a beer.

"No, I'm going. And I won't be coming back. I'm done."

That finally caught his attention.

He put the bottle down on the counter and looked at me, before grinning that smug grin of his he'd developed recently. "That's funny Jess, but seriously, where are you off out to?"

"I'm not going out, I'm leaving. Full stop. We're over Liam."

"But... but you have to be joking. I mean, it's not logical for you to go - where are you going to go? You don't even have a job."

Even though it was perfectly true, that point really stung. "It doesn't matter. I've sorted something. My bags are in the car ready to go. I've left my key over there."

"Car? You don't have a car. Why are you doing this Jess? I love you."

He moved towards me, arms outstretched but I moved away from him. If I let him get too close, he could easily crack my defences and worm his way through. "I've borrowed the car. And I'm leaving because it seems that even though you supposedly love me, you'd rather sleep with Lara from your office."

He opened and closed his mouth a few times, not quite sure how he could explain that, but he clearly knew he couldn't get away with denying it now so he tried to justify it instead.

"It...it only happened the once Jess and I feel so bad about it. I haven't even seen her in over a month. I was drunk, it meant nothing. I love *you*."

Well, that was another lie because I'd seen him with her a week ago. I was almost certain that when he'd been "working late" on Valentine's Day a fortnight ago, he was actually with her. Not that I could prove anything.

His phone started to ring and he pulled it out of his pocket, staring at it in obvious horror before hitting the ignore button. "Er, Dan from work. It can wait, it won't be important."

I would stake my life on that being Lara, not Dan. But I'd had enough. It was time to go. "Goodbye Liam. I hope everything works out for you."

I walked out of the flat while he was still shouting excuses at me. I took the stairs two at a time to get myself out to the car and locked the doors as soon as I was inside. Liam wasn't far behind me and was trying to open the door whilst shouting at me. I ignored him and pulled the car out of its space, driving until I couldn't see him in the rear-view mirror anymore. It was only then that I started to cry, but somewhere amid the tears of sadness, I think there was a couple of joy and relief.

Chapter 2

By the time I had made it back to Gran's, the tears had completely subsided. The more distance I put between myself and London, the more I knew I was doing the right thing. Getting stuck in traffic for an hour on the M25 gave me a lot of time to reflect and I didn't like what I came up with. I stopped feeling upset and began to feel angry. Partly at Liam for what he had done, but mostly for myself for how pathetic I had become. I'm not even sure how it happened because I wasn't always such a pushover. The change must have happened subtly, but over a long period. No more. I had a chance to start over and I was going to do it properly. I was going to start doing what I wanted, get a job that I would love and hopefully, once I was back on my feet, a boyfriend who was even better than Liam. It was petty, but I wanted to be able to turn around one day and be able to flaunt everything in Liam's face, making him regret humiliating me.

Gran was already at the door by the time I pulled up on the drive and was out to get my things before I'd even turned the engine off.

"Did everything go ok? Did he make a fuss and try lying to you?" she asked as I climbed out of the car.

"Something like that. Gran, don't you dare pick those boxes up. You can take the bin liner but that's it."

She gave me a stubborn look but sensibly thought better against contradicting me. "I've moved some things about in the bigger of the two spare rooms. Turns out we had a bed under all those boxes." Her mouth twitched. "I'm afraid you'll have to make do as it is for tonight and we'll have a proper sort out tomorrow. You can redecorate it however you want. Lord knows the last time that room was actually painted."

I stacked the two boxes on top of each other and closed the car door with my hip. "Really Gran, I don't want to be any trouble."

I couldn't see her face because the boxes blocking my view, but I could guess her expression just by the tone of her voice. "Jessica, you are not a lodger in my house, you are my granddaughter and we will make that room yours and you will feel at home here. Do I make myself clear?"

I suddenly felt five-years old. "Yes Gran."

"Good. Now let's put your stuff away and I will make you some dinner."

I grudgingly followed behind her with my boxes, completely aware that if I let her, she was going to completely spoil me and I would never want to leave her house. I wouldn't entirely be surprised if she started to give me pocket money again, but I was going to have to put my foot down there.

The following morning, after a proper full English breakfast that Gran insisted I eat all of (apparently I was looking too skinny these days), we set about making a start on the spare room. Gran's house had three bedrooms but since it had been just her and Grandad, the extra bedrooms had mainly been used for storage. Because of all the extra boxes, it had been easier for me to sleep on an airbed while my parents had the spare bed that wasn't covered with things. All this had only really occurred over the last couple of years since they'd had an issue with the floorboards in their loft and had to have them all replaced. The boxes from the loft had been moved into the spare rooms and Grandad had just never gotten around to putting them back.

Armed with a fresh cup of tea, Gran stood in the doorway of the bedroom and surveyed the boxes. She was dressed in an old floral day dress I recognised as the one she tended to wear when she did the gardening and her hair was pulled into a very tight French plait.

"I don't think anything should be too dusty, but you never know so watch yourself. If we start here," she said, indicating the boxes nearest to her, "then work our way to the other end of the room. I think a lot of it we can probably donate to a charity shop or just chuck because it's bound to be mostly junk."

I pulled the hairband off my wrist and tied my hair into a ponytail, ready to get started.

Gran wasn't wrong. There really was quite a bit of junk. We even stumbled across what looked like old car parts that Gran couldn't understand why Grandad had felt the need to keep these in the loft. Needless to say, she put these straight into the junk pile to be thrown out after tutting at his hording. It took us most of the morning to go through the first half of the room and we ended up with a good pile of things to throw and a good number of lamps and figurines to pass on to charity shops. After a quick round of sandwiches for lunch, we set to work on the second half and this was when we stumbled across the treasure trove.

I opened one of the boxes and found a mountain of perfectly preserved clothes, individually wrapped in tissue paper and the faint scent of lavender coming out of the box. I pulled the top item from the box and carefully peeled away the paper, standing up to unfurl it. It was a beautiful lemon coloured fifties-style prom dress with a nipped in waist and a circle skirt.

Gran's face immediately lit up when she saw it. "Oh, I remember that dress. That was the dress I wore on my first date with your grandfather. It took me over a month to get it just right and I felt like it was the perfect opportunity to show it off."

"You made this?" I knew Gran liked to sew and she was always doing craft bits and pieces but I had no idea how talented she actually was.

"Of course. Back then, I liked to make most of my own clothes. I had this crazy notion in my head that I could be the next Coco Chanel when I was younger."

I sat myself down on the edge of the bed, still holding the dress in my hands. "Why didn't you? I don't know much about fashion but I know enough to see that this is perfectly made."

She sat herself down next to me on the bed. "I don't think I ever pursued it hard enough. Maybe I was scared about failing, so I never pushed myself to actively do it. I just thought if it was meant to be, it was meant to be, but I still enjoyed sewing regardless of who I was making the clothes for."

I started to unpack the rest of the clothes from the box. This must have been how pirates felt when they found buried treasure. Every dress, skirt and shirt I took out from the tissue paper was more beautiful than the last. With each item, Gran's eyes grew brighter and she seemed to remember the clothing and something she was doing when she was wearing it. Each piece had its own individual tale.

Under the box was a trunk that I flipped open to reveal more treasure. Rolls of fabric in all kinds of different patterns. It made Gran's face just light up and she started to lift the fabric out of the trunk, running her hand lovingly across it.

"Gran, I think you need to start dressmaking again." I stated quietly as she picked out another roll of flowy material.

It took her a second to respond to me. "You know, I think I probably could. This material has held out really well considering how long it has been locked in that trunk. But I can't make anything for myself any more. I can make things for you! In fact, most of these clothes will probably already fit you."

As she picked up a sky-blue dress from the bed and held it against me to get an idea about the fit, I tried to cut across her. "Gran, really don't go to all the -."

"Jess, don't say it's going to be too much trouble. What else am I going to do with my time? I'd like to do it. God knows you bought hardly any clothes with you and they were all either black, grey or white. You could do with injecting some colour into your wardrobe."

I really couldn't argue with her there. My wardrobe was probably as pathetic as I was at the moment. I sighed, knowing she wasn't going to let this one go and part of me glad that she wasn't. "Ok Gran, I'll do you a deal. I'll take on the clothes you've already got here and will maybe accept a couple of newly made items, but you have to find some time to teach me to sew as well."

It seemed I'd struck onto a good idea. "Jess, I would love that. I used to get together with my friends when I was younger and we'd sit around gossiping and sewing."

"Could you not start something like that again?"

"Well, I think I could persuade a couple of women to come over once a week if I promise that cake will be involved too."

"Excellent, and I can join you and that's how you can teach me how to sew."

The smile on Gran's face convinced me that I had suggested the right thing. I already knew I was going to be awful and I would end up pricking myself with a needle so many times I would probably lose all sense of feeling in my fingers, but if it meant spending time with her, it would all be worth it.

"I'll ring around later and find out if anyone is interested. But for now, go try this dress on and I'll see if I need to alter it."

And so the remaining boxes lay forgotten and I spent the rest of the day being fitted for my whole new wardrobe full off Elsie Crawford originals.

Chapter 3

Dressed in a red pencil dress, a Gran original from the fifties, and armed with multiple copies of my CV, I walked the two miles into town to make a start on sorting my life out. I had been in Pickney for a week already and it was time to get my arse in gear. The walk itself started to help. As I walked against the chilly February wind, I felt it blow away the cobwebs and smog London had covered me in.

A fresh start.

I wasn't exactly sure what I was going to do with my life but I knew that I needed a job. At the moment, I wasn't going to be fussy if I could get something that was full time and paid semi-decently. And after doing the rounds with any recruitment agency that I came across and practically forcing them to let me register with them, I felt more positive about my career than I had in a very long time. At least I was being assertive and putting myself out there. And all that assertiveness was making me hungry, so when I caught the whiff of the delicious aroma coming out of the Italian restaurant called Amato's that I happened to be passing, I decided to treat myself to lunch. It was even better when I saw they had a two-course lunch menu for a tenner. I had definitely earned it.

I was greeted by a relatively grumpy-looking waiter who was probably a few years younger than me and really looked like he didn't want to be there. He sat me down at a little table set for two and left me with a menu before skulking off without a word. As long as the food tasted as good as it smelt, I could probably cope with the bad service.

I must have caught the back end of the lunch rush as the place was quickly emptying out save for a woman on the table next to me, who was also eating alone, along with a couple of men dressed in work clothes and a dark-haired woman sat at the bar. I couldn't see her face, but she was laughing with one of the servers behind the bar and her warm laugh was carrying right to the back of the restaurant.

Eventually my waiter returned and asked me to order. He didn't ask me if I was ready to order, he actually told me to order. I thought I heard the woman on the table next to me tut while she seemed to be working through a stack of papers in front of her. Keeping it simple, I ordered a bottle of still water along with the tomato and mozzarella salad, followed with spaghetti bolognese. He returned a couple of minutes later with a bottle of water that I only realised wasn't still when he had unscrewed the top and was pouring it into a glass for me.

"Erm, I'm sorry but I ordered still water not sparkling."

His eyes flashed to me as if he was trying to work out why I had even dared to point out his mistake. "It's water."

I wasn't exactly good with confrontation and if I actually liked sparkling water, I would have accepted it without a word and drank the bottle. But I hated sparkling water and he was being very rude about the whole thing. "Yes, but its sparkling water and I ordered still."

"And you can't drink it anyway? It's water," he replied as if I was asking him to give me one of his vital organs.

"No, I don't like sparkling water."

"So you're going to pay for another bottle?"

I was on the verge of really losing it with him. What on earth was wrong with this place? But I was saved from the unwanted argument by the woman on the table next to me.

Her chair scrapped back loudly and stood up so she was next to me, glaring at the waiter. She had a perfectly cut brown bob and was obviously pregnant. But then she was very slim and petite, so it was quite possible she wasn't as far along as I thought but her bump just looked bigger on her tiny frame.

"This lady ordered a still water because I heard her order it. And what's more, so did you and you are the one who made the mistake here." There was a steely tone to her voice that immediately made me admire and respect her, as well as telling me she was someone who shouldn't be crossed. "If anyone should pay for the new bottle, it should be you considering it was your error and you're the one being so rude about it. I demand to speak to the manager now. I want to make a complaint about you and your attitude. Now."

Our waiter had just been staring blankly at her, clearly blinded by the authoritative aura she was exuding but he seemed to have picked out the words "manager" and "complaint" because he started to look worried. He didn't even have a chance to respond to my defender because his name, well I assumed it was his name because someone shouted "Daniel!" in an angry tone, and our waiter jumped as if he'd been electrocuted.

I only caught a glimpse of the man who shouted at our waiter before he walked back to some hidden part of the restaurant. He was dark-haired and had been wearing chef's whites, so I got the impression that Daniel was going to be in trouble now.

He slumped off towards the staff-only part of the restaurant and I looked up at the woman next to me, a little taken aback that her seriousness had completely dissolved and she was smiling at me.

"Thank you. I never would have been able to handle it that well."

She waved a hand through the air as if what she had just done had been no disruption to her quiet lunch whatsoever. "Not a problem at all. Do you mind I sit with you? I'm not really in the mood for a solitary lunch."

"Erm, sure."

She smiled brightly, picked her papers up from her own table then sat in the chair opposite me. "Thanks. It's not even half-two and we've already managed to get an inept waiter sacked from his job. It seems like a pretty productive day to me."

I wasn't sure if she was trying to make a joke or if she revelled in the idea of having people sacked. "I feel a bit bad for him though."

"I wouldn't feel too guilty about it if I were you; he was an awful waiter and was on his final chance anyway. He should have been sacked weeks ago if you ask me. Mind if I join you too?"

I looked up to the woman speaking to me and had to do a double take. She looked like a complete dead ringer for Monica Bellucci at her peak. Long, thick black hair framed her perfectly symmetrical face, the main focus of which was large, brown eyes. And she had a body to die for in a figure-hugging sun dress, despite the cold weather outside, complete with sky-high heels. I'd never felt so self-conscious of my own appearance in all my life. In a million years my body would never fill out a dress like hers did and I couldn't walk five metres in heels without stacking.

She hadn't waited for me to answer her question and was already shifting the small table next to us to form a double table and sat herself down next to the woman with the bob, extending her hand out for introductions. "I'm Lucy by the way."

I shook her hand, completely in awe of the confidence oozing from her. It was almost as intimidating as the confidence the woman opposite me had displayed when giving the waiter what for. "I'm Jess."

"And I'm Ashley," said my brunette champion.

"Lovely to meet you ladies. You've already made my very dull day much more exciting, so thank you for that."

A new waiter, who looked much friendlier than the man who had dealt with me before, now stood next to our table. "Ladies, we're sorry for the inconvenience Daniel caused by just generally being the massive knob he is, so drinks are on us today. Expect for you Lucy – you weren't involved to start with plus I hear you still have that drinking problem."

She obviously must be a regular since the waiter knew her name and she laughed at his comment. "Oh Graham, I never expect to get anything free in this place. But I'll have a glass of merlot anyway please."

"I suppose that'll be alright. Anything for either of you ladies?"

Ashley ordered another orange juice and I went mad with a glass of rosé, seeing as it was going to be free anyway. We had already ordered our food separately, but the waiter told us he'd make sure he'd bring it all over at the same time now we were sat together.

Lucy attempted to cross her legs over under the table but accidentally kicked my shopping bags over. "Oh I'm really sorry." She got off her chair and started to stand them back upright. "What have you been on a spending spree for, if you don't mind me asking?"

"Well, my gran is really into sewing and she's starting up a sewing bee, so I wanted to go out and get my own supplies. I ended up getting distracted and buying quite a bit of really nice fabric I probably can't afford. I don't know why I bought it because I don't even know how to sew."

"That's fantastic!" Lucy's smile seemed big enough to light up the entire room. "When's this sewing bee? Can anyone come? I've always wanted to learn how to make my own stuff but I haven't had time until now."

"I think it's pretty much an open invitation. So far Gran has just asked a couple of her friends to come, so I'm sure she'll enjoy having more people there."

"Can I come too? I really need to learn how sew. And cook. She isn't doing cooking lessons either is she?" Both Lucy and I looked at Ashley with what must have been the same quizzical look, so she elaborated. "You might have guessed that I'm pregnant." She rested her hands on her neat little bump. "I can't do anything domesticated. Like, at all. I want to make sure that I know how to do the little things that mums should be able to do."

That seemed like a really nice notion to me. "Of course you can come too. And Gran is an excellent cook, she'd probably be more than happy to give you lessons."

"It seems like meeting you in here today was fate." she said with a bright smile.

"Agreed," Lucy stated, lifting her wine glass. "As Rick said, *Louie, I think this could be the beginning of a beautiful friendship.*"

We all chinked our glasses and the confidence in my decision to move to Pitney only strengthened. I was still unemployed, but I already had more of a social life than I had in London.

Our starters all arrived at the same time and I dug straight into the mozzarella, feeling famished from the excitement of the afternoon. With a mouthful of food, I tried to answer Lucy's questions about my grandmother. She was very interested in her sewing history and I was trying my best to pass on the facts.

"How long has she been sewing for then?"

"Most of her life. When she was younger, she made a lot of her own clothes. She made this dress actually."

I gestured to my pencil dress and her interest lit up her face. "Really? Stand up and let me see." I stood up to give her a better look and gave a little twirl when she asked me to, even though I felt ridiculous doing it. "It's so beautiful. Was your gran a designer or something?"

"No," I replied as I took my seat again, "although I found out the other day that she would have liked to have done that. Honestly, I knew she was good but I never knew she was this good. She's always just done this for fun."

"I can't wait to meet your gran," Lucy beamed. "I've always wanted to be good at something creative. I was an accountant until I got made redundant a couple of months back after a massive shake up and there's no room for creatively in finance. Well, there is, but if you're getting creative then you're probably doing something illegal."

"Redundancy is awful. Have you found anything else yet?" Ashley asked.

"No, but I'm not really looking to be honest. I'm trying to work out what I want to do with my life beyond spreadsheets and calculators. I'm just in that weird kind of No Man's Land at the moment."

"I can empathise," I piped up. "I've just moved from London and haven't had a chance to do what I really want in years. I used to love my job, helping people start up new businesses because it was really rewarding to see everything to come together, but I followed my boyfriend to London and ended up temping just to get money. Now I'm having to start all over again."

"Well, while we're sharing, let me add to the therapy session. I was a complete workaholic when I worked as a marketing exec in London but we've just moved out here after I found out I was pregnant because I couldn't keep working like I was and remain healthy. Now I've gone from twelve-hour days to no-hour days and I'm struggling to know what to do with myself."

"Well it looks like The Universe has thrown us all together since we're in the same boat," Lucy laughed. "I imagine we're going to be seeing a lot of each other from now on, so we better make a date for our first sewing bee."

Chapter 4

The night finally arrived for the inaugural Sewing Bee and I was feeling unexplainable pressure for it to be a good night. Gran had managed to round up a couple of friends and I had Lucy and Ashley, both of whom were apparently very excited. They'd both told me so numerous times over our group chat, entitled *Sew What?*, that Lucy had started up after we'd all exchanged numbers. But the thread had quickly moved from confirming what time they should show up to general chit chat and the occasional meme. Even though it was through a phone screen, our conversations flowed easily and I found myself liking these women more and more. Since they both had high expectations for the evening, I didn't want to let them down.

The doorbell rang at seven and I practically leapt out of my seat to answer the door, only to find it was Dorothy, one of Gran's friends.

"Oh Jessica, so lovely to see you again," she practically sang as she stepped past me to get into the house. "You're looking so grown up these days."

I gave her a kiss on the papery cheek she offered me. Despite looking very much her eighty-nine years, she was a very spritely old dear who always had a twinkle in her eye and an inappropriate comment on her tongue. Plus, she seemed to have brought fresh home-baked goods with her, which made me like her even more.

She instantly made herself at home in the living room, being very familiar with the layout of the house since she had been friends with Gran for over forty years.

Gran had set up a sewing area around the coffee table for her friends and had opened the dividing doors to the dining room so I could work at the table with my new friends, but Gran could still keep an eye on us. It seemed we, as the novices, would be taking it more seriously whereas the experts were just bringing some sewing they needed to get done, but would be able to gossip and drink tea whilst doing it in comfort.

To her immense credit, my grandmother had taken her role as Sewer-In-Chief very seriously when it came to the new recruits. She had spent the afternoon going through her fabric collection and planning what we could do as the beginners group to get into the swing of things. Her lesson plan was going to be to show us some different types of stitches for the first half and for the second she would set us a small project.

The next person to ring the doorbell was Gran's friend Olive, who had brought her granddaughter's Brownie sash with her and was going to use the evening to unpick all the "terrible stitches" on the badges her daughter-in-law had already sewn and re-do them so they looked presentable.

"She's one of those working mothers," Olive explained, highlighting the difference in the generational ideals. "Can't sew to save her life. Or clean, come to think of it. She has a woman come into her house and clean for her."

"We can't be good at everything Olive," Gran replied patiently then swiftly changed the subject. "What did your granddaughter get this badge for?"

When the doorbell went again, it was Lucy and Ashley. Lucy greeted me with a very European double-cheek kiss but I had learnt through our group chat that she was of Italian heritage and her brother actually owned the restaurant we had all met in.

"Ask Ashley to show you the contents of her bag," Lucy said with a mischievous smile as they followed me to our sewing table.

"I like to be prepared," Ashely replied defensively.

As she unpacked her bag onto the table, I had to smother my own laugh; she really did like to be prepared. She had brought five books on sewing with her.

"Have you read them yet?" I asked.

"I have a lot of spare time during the day now I don't work."

I took that as she had read all five of them.

"Evening ladies," Gran said as she reached the table, extending a plate of fresh Madeira cake. "First rule of the sewing bee – sugar makes your sewing better."

"This is going to be my type of learning," Lucy smiled as she grabbed a slice.

Gran set the plate down on the table and took a seat in the empty chair next to Ashley and picked up a needle, threading it first time to prove what a pro she was. "So, we're going to start you all off with the basics. You can practice some stitches for a while and then I thought I'd let you make your own needle cases from some of this felt here so you have something to take home with you. The first stitch I'm going to show you is the running stitch, which is one of the first things you need to learn as all the other stitches are based on this in one way or another. It's essentially the foundation stitch and you'd use it when making basic seams if you're making your own clothing."

I stifled a smile as Lucy and Ashley nodded silently with rapt attention. They were definitely taking this a lot more seriously than I was. I was just glad to be doing something social on a Tuesday evening instead of being sat alone in the flat with whatever terrible reality show was on TV as my only company.

I forced myself to concentrate as Gran began her demonstration. "I'd suggest using about eighteen inches of thread for each practice run and make sure you knot the end or you'll be continually pulling it out and having to restart. With this stitch, you can either sew it or stab it through the fabric; just go with whatever feels easier for you. I prefer sewing it, which is where you scoop up a little bit of the fabric as you go along and the scoop is what makes the gap between the stitches." We watched silently as she demonstrated. "But the stabbing method is literally just up and down through the fabric." She then demonstrated this method to us as well.

It all looked pretty straight forward. The needle goes into the fabric, leave a little bit of a gap, bring it up again and then push it back through the back, making a stitch. Easy peasy.

Famous last words.

"So have a play around with that and then when you feel comfortable with that, you can try a backstitch which is good for sturdier seams. With this stitch, you put your needle into the fabric, like so, bring it through the back, but now you start the new stitch where the old stitch ended and work along the row. As you can see, this method means you don't have any gaps between the stitches which is what makes it sturdier. Make sense?"

We all nodded silently at our teacher who just smiled back at us. "But you'll never learn until you do so it's time to dive in ladies. I'll just be over there if you have any trouble, otherwise I'll check on you in a little while and we can make a start on your needle cases. I'll show you how to do a blanket stitch for those as it looks much nicer when decorating it."

Running stitch. Backstitch. Blanket stitch. I should probably start writing these down so I remembered them. Although a quick glance at Ashley told me she was doing just that. Maybe I could just copy her notes. Was Gran planning to set us a test afterwards?

We fell into a comfortable silence for a few minutes as both Ashley and Lucy moved through their running stitch with ruthless efficiency, the concentration etched on their faces. Me? I was concentrating just as much but it wasn't exactly what you'd call efficient. It seemed wherever I stuck the needle, it came up in a part of the fabric I didn't want it to. If this was just the basics, I was stuffed.

Gran kept her word and let us get on with it, but the same couldn't be said for her friends. They kept coming over to see how we were getting on, like we were some kind of sewing zoo commodity, and imparting their wisdom on us, pointing out where we were going wrong. Though the latter seemed to be aimed more at me because I was the only one not getting it straight away.

"Dear, with a good running stitch the key is to be consistent in the size of the stitches and the intervals. Yours are all over the place," Olive had commented helpfully. "But before we sort those out, we must get you some more cake. You're all skin and bones."

Eventually Gran had to step in and subtly get Olive back into her own circle, though not before I got my slice of cake.

"This must be a very different Tuesday night for a twenty-something who used to live in London," Ashely pointed out.

"Very, but not how you think. This is probably the most rock and roll night I've had in a long time," I replied with a wry smile.

"Really?"

"Afraid so."

"There's a story that goes with that frown," Ashely guessed correctly.

I sighed. "It's a story that doesn't paint me in the best light."

"Come on, you can tell us," Lucy prompted. "We're all friends here and we're in a sewing bee together. Surely there's some kind of bond between us now? You could tell us you killed someone and we'd have to keep quiet because that's what Sewing Sisters do."

Ashley and I laughed at the serious look on Lucy's face, though she wasn't able to hold it for very long and she began laughing with us. "You don't have to tell us Jess but just know, I have this theory stuck in my head that you're being hunted down for an assassination attempt on the Queen and that's why you're hiding out in Pickney."

"I wish it was as interesting as that. No, it's just a simple, cliché-ridden girl meets boy story."

So I preceded to fill them in on the last couple of years of my life, leaving home for London when Liam got his job because he asked me to and then not being able to find steady work, how I was essentially some kind of hermit and how my lovely boyfriend subtly began to change to the point I didn't recognise him anymore and he started cheating on me but kept me around because I was the mug that cleaned his flat and ran his errands since he was too busy to do anything himself. By the end of our relationship, I had basically become his housekeeper.

"What a dick," Lucy said with such vehemence that my heart swelled a little. She didn't even know him but she already had my back.

"I can't believe he wouldn't even take time off to go to your grandfather's funeral. Even I wouldn't have done that and I hardly ever used my holiday entitlement until Ryan had to actually threaten to divorce me unless I had a few days off."

"Thanks guys. But what's done is done and I'm kind of glad I did something about it in the end. Gran had to force me into doing something about it or I would probably still be there, playing the role of a human doormat. It's weird but I already feel more confident about my life in a couple of weeks in Pickney than I did at any point in London, even if I am still unemployed."

"At least you listened to her advice," Ashley said. "And I'm glad you did otherwise we wouldn't have met you and I wouldn't be here. The job thing will pick up, don't worry about that."

"That's something I want to know too," Lucy began. "How does a high-power Marketing exec in London get excited about a Tuesday night sewing bee in a stranger's kitchen?"

"It's always interested me," she said quickly. A little too quickly.

I glanced over at Lucy and we both raised an eyebrow at the same time. "I don't buy it for a second. Come on, I had to be honest. You said the other day you wanted to learn because of the baby? Sewing isn't a requirement for raising a child, so there's something else to it."

She sighed and her face fell slightly, making me incredibly guilty for pushing her. "I'm just worried I'm going to be a terrible mother."

Her comment surprised me so much that I had a momentary lapse in concentration and stabbed the needle into my thumb. "Ow! How could you even think that? The fact you already care so much says you're going to be a great mum."

Ashley set her fabric gently on the table. "I didn't have the greatest mother. She had a drink problem and made some really bad choices. I ended up getting taken away by Social Services when I was ten and spent the next eight years in and out of foster homes."

"Oh Ash, that's awful. What happened to your mum? Did she not fight to get you back?" Lucy asked.

"She died a year after I was taken away. A drug overdose apparently. Maybe she started using after I left which meant maybe she did care in some way. Although I'd much prefer it if she'd cleaned her act up," she said through a shaky laugh.

"You poor thing. But that doesn't mean *you're* going to be a bad mum."

Ashley let out a sigh. "I know. But at the back of my mind, I can't help thinking that I'm going to fail somehow. I almost did already. Do you know why I left my job and moved here?"

I glanced over at Lucy before we both silently shook our heads.

"I collapsed because I was working myself too hard. I was used to working as many hours as I could cram into the day but I started to get tired. I ignored it and just started drinking more coffee. Then one day, I was leading a presentation in front of some important clients and my boss. I started to feel dizzy, but it was too important, so I pushed on. Everything went black and the next thing I knew, I was lying in a hospital bed. That was when I found out I was pregnant."

"But you didn't know you were pregnant," I protested. "Maybe you should have eased up a little for the sake of your own health generally, but you weren't intentionally putting your child at risk. And everything is ok now, isn't it?"

"Thankfully yes, but I could have really done some damage. When I pictured having kids, I always wanted them to have what I didn't. They were going to grow up in a two-parent family, in a nice house with a mother who would cook their dinner and help make their school play costumes. I want to be a good mum, but -."

"But nothing," Lucy cut across, reaching over to Ashley and giving her hand a squeeze. "It's all ok now and you're going to be a fantastic mum. Your child is definitely going to have the best Halloween and school theme day costumes if you keep sewing like you are."

Ashley started to laugh and a couple of stray tears she had been fighting back fell down her cheeks. "Thanks. I really appreciate it. I'm so glad your brother hires really incompetent staff or I never would have met you both."

"Me too," Lucy smiled. "Although I don't think it was part of Rob's plan to hire incompetent staff. Hopefully whoever he gets next will be a bit better."

"Hear, hear," I said before turning my attention back to the fabric so I didn't stab my finger again. I wasn't a natural but I was enjoying the atmosphere. "What's your story then Luce? You seemed more excited than a normal person should be about a sewing bee in a stranger's house on a Tuesday evening too. You said you wanted to learn to make your own clothes?"

For the first time since I had met her, the bright aura surrounding her seemed to dim and her confident mask slipped ever so slightly. "Please don't laugh but I'd always had this dream of selling them, maybe owning my own shop. All the kinds of vintage fashions your Gran used to make."

"Why would we laugh? That sounds pretty reasonable to me."

"Maybe, but I wonder if twenty-nine is a bit too late to start this up. Now would be a good a time as any. Being made redundant was a pain at first but it made me realise I hated being an accountant. Along with a decent pay-out which we haven't had to touch because John's job just about covers all our outgoings, I have money tucked away from when my parents died a few years ago. I think I could use it as start-up money and I know my parents would have liked me to use the money on something that wasn't boring. My brother actually used his share to set up his restaurant. I also know John would be fully supportive if I decided to go ahead with it but I feel like I'm gambling with our future. I mean, we're getting married, so shouldn't I be more sensible and go back to doing something I know will give me a steady wage?"

"Not if you hate doing it," Ashley answered. "Life isn't all about working, trust me on this one."

"She's right. If you can afford to give it a go and John's going to support you, why shouldn't you follow your dream?"

"I've only just started sewing though."

I looked down at the fabric she was working on then held mine next to it, so she could see the comparison. Where my stitches looked like they'd been sewn by a blind person who had five thumbs on each hand, Lucy's were sewing machine perfect. If anyone was a natural at this, then it was her.

"Speak to Gran and see if she'll give you some extra lessons," I suggested. "She'll be more than happy to and if you're not working at the minute, you can do it during the day with her."

"Really?" Lucy's face lit up with excitement. "Do you think she'd mind? How much would she charge for private lessons?"

I started to laugh at the picture in my head. "Don't even suggest paying her or she'll stab you with her needles. I think she'll enjoy the company and also the chance to pass on her skills since it's obvious I'm not getting anywhere with this."

To prove my point, I lifted the fabric I'd attempted some more stitches on and dropped it, but instead of falling to the floor it just dangled. Somehow I had managed to sew it to the sleeve of my jumper without even noticing until now. On the bright side, I had avoided making contact with the skin on my wrist, so I was going to put it in the win column.

As the girls looked at the limp fabric hanging from my sleeve, we all burst out laughing, unable to stop for a solid minute. As I wiped a tear away, I made eye contact with Gran and she smiled at me. In that second I realised that this wasn't about the sewing anymore, it was about so much more than that.

Chapter 5

Knocking on the door of Lucy's house, I gripped at the wine bottle in my hand, feeling slightly nervous. Being in Pickney had already given me more of a social life than I had in London and I was now about to go to my first proper dinner party in forever.

When I had, on the rare occasion, ventured out with Liam and some of his friends and their partners, we usually went to some bar with ridiculously overpriced drinks or a restaurant with tiny portions. We never went into anyone's home and they never came into ours.

Now, after two weeks' worth of sewing bees, I seemed to actually have friends again. Two women who were clever, successful and lovely. Two women who I would be proud to call my friends. It was almost like first date jitters but this was much, much more important than just some first date.

The door swung open and Lucy stood in front of me, looking her usual radiant self in a tight dress that highlighted her perfect hour-glass shape. "Jess! Come in." I handed her the bottle of wine as I stepped into the house and she pulled me in for a hug. "Thanks. Come on through. We're almost ready to eat."

It seemed I was the last one to arrive, which wasn't the best start. Had I been holding everyone up?

I followed Lucy into the living-cum-dining room to see four other people sat around the large table that took up half the room. The only one of the four I actually recognised was Ashley, who smiled at me as soon as I stepped into the room.

"For everyone who doesn't know, this is Jess," Lucy announced brightly. "Jess, this is John, then there's Ashley's husband Ryan and finally my brother, Rob."

I smiled as each of them was introduced and I received a smile in return from all of them except Lucy's brother. Instead, he just gave me a cool nod before turning a hard stare onto his sister. I could definitely see a family resemblance and apparently their family had been at the front of the queue when it came to the attractive gene. Like Lucy, he had jet-black hair, large liquid-chocolate eyes and enviably sharp cheekbones. But whereas Lucy's face always seemed on the verge of a smile, her brother had a much more serious look to him, as if his lips weren't quite used to tilting upwards.

"Jess, take a seat. Dinner's almost ready and you're going to love it. It's an old family recipe from my nonna, completely secret to anyone outside the Amato clan," Lucy said as her eyes sparkled with their usual happiness.

I took the empty seat next to her brother and made another attempt at being friendly since I was going to be sat next to him all evening. "I'm guessing you're the brother with the restaurant? I love it there, your food's great."

Instead of looking pleased with the compliment he just nodded his head again. "Thanks."

Then the awkward silence set in and I wasn't sure what else to say to him. I got the impression that whatever I asked him, I was only going to get one word answers. Thankfully Ashley jumped in to save the day.

"Jess, how did the interview yesterday go?"

"Good I think. It seemed like a nice place to work and they're going to let me know. Although Gran is being a complete pain at the moment. I got a job offer the other day and when I explained what it entailed, she essentially emotionally blackmailed me into turning it down."

Ashley started to laugh. "Your grandmother is one tough cookie. But why did she make you turn it down?"

"She thought it sounded too dull and I should be doing something I loved. She told me to continue to be picky."

"Smart lady," Ashley's husband Ryan said as he raised his wine glass. "There's no point doing something in this world if it doesn't make you happy. Life's too short."

"True dat!" John replied, knocking his own glass against Ryan's in agreement.

Neither of my new friend's partners were what I'd pictured at all. Ashley was petite and always immaculately put together whereas Ryan was about a foot taller than her, built like a rugby player and had a more rugged look going on. I remembered Ashley saying that he ran his own business where he built furniture, so he was more of a hands-on person – quite the opposite of the previous city exec his wife had been. Though considering the way he looked at Ashley, there was no doubt how much he loved her.

"What is you do John?" I asked, wondering if he was doing a job he enjoyed too.

"I'm a Web Designer. Yep, complete IT geek," he added with an apologetic shrug, "but I love what I do."

He did have a little bit of a geeky vibe going on and I wouldn't have immediately picked him as Lucy's fiancé if he was in a room filled with other men, but being with him in person made me see why they were so suited. He came across as incredibly laid-back and had a very easy, welcoming smile that matched Lucy's perfectly since she was one of those people who always seemed to have a smile on her face too. Plus, he was incredibly cute, in a John Krasinski kind of way.

"Are you with a company or self-employed?" Ryan asked. "Ash has been telling me for ages I need to modernise my website but the guy I used before charged an arm and a leg. Wondered if I could get mate's rates now our women-folk are friends, which means we're obviously going to be forced to be friends as well."

Everyone except Lucy's brother started to laugh and banter began flying around the table, along with John's promise he would look at Ryan's website for a very competitive rate. Though it was a new group, to me it felt like we had known each other for years. It was already surprising how well I was getting on with Lucy and Ashley after such a short time, but throwing their partners into the mix too and having everyone get on so well was something I was unused to. Well, everyone except Rob who never offered up a smile and didn't really get involved with any of the conversation unless he had to.

"Here we go, Nonna Celia's famous spinach and cheese manicotti," Lucy sang as she made her way back into the room and placed the dish in the middle of the table. "There's three for everyone so dig in. And help yourself to salad and bread."

"It looks and smells amazing Luce," I said as I immediately started to load my plate. "I feel a little spoilt having a proper home-cooked Italian meal."

"If you were having a proper Italian meal I would be serving you five courses and there would be a lot more salt in everything. And we'd be starting to eat about two hours from now."

"Now you know why I'm marrying her. It's all about her excellent cooking skills," John joked. "So Jess, back to the work conundrum – what's been your favourite job so far? Let's try and get you something your Gran will approve on and then we can crack on with sorting out that crisis in the Middle East before dessert."

I laughed at John before giving it some real thought. "I loved what I did before I moved to London. I worked for a company that helped people set up small businesses, giving them all the start-up information they needed and then supporting them while they found their footing. But I haven't been able to find any vacancies for anything like that around here, so it looks like a no-go at the moment. Otherwise, I'd probably have to say waitressing."

"Really? You were a waitress?" Lucy asked.

"Yeah. When I was at school I did weekends at the village pub and through Uni I worked at a really great burger place. I always liked the hectic nature of the job, being on your feet instead of at a desk. But it's probably mostly because I lucked out at both places and worked with some great people. If you get on with who you work with, it really makes the job."

"I'm a genius!" John declared to the table as he slammed down his cutlery.

"We know that *tesoro* but do you want to enlighten us why so this time?" Lucy asked with a grin.

"Rob, you need a new member on the serving team at the restaurant now you're shot of Daniel and

Jess needs a job and has experience as a waitress. Do you both see where I'm coming from here?"

"John, you *are* a genius!" Lucy leaned in to kiss his cheek. "That's such a brilliant idea I'm annoyed I didn't think of it myself."

By the looks of it, Rob didn't share their enthusiasm, instead he just shrugged as he poured himself another glass of wine. I felt a little insulted because I had been a very good waitress in my time and he had no right to assume I was anything other than a pro. Not that I was too keen to work for someone like him. I might be desperate but I still had some standards.

"Rob, don't make that face. You know full well that you need to replace Daniel soon. Tina is a working mum so she can't take on the extra shifts and the guys will only do it for a while before they start complaining."

"Fine, if she wants to apply for a job she can."

"*She* is sitting right next to you so you're perfectly able to turn your head and talk to her yourself," I blurted out angrily.

A silence immediately fell on the table and I felt the heat rise in my cheeks. I was definitely not the confrontational type but something about Lucy's brother and the way he was acting had really riled me up.

Rob actually did turn to look at me and he seemed more than a little surprised at my outburst. I'm not sure if it was just wishful thinking, but I'm sure I saw a glimmer of guilt on his face. "Ok. If you want to apply, then you can. Just give Lucy your info and I'll see what I can do."

He turned his attention back to his food and that was it. I wasn't sure what I'd done to offend him, since we'd only just met, but I had the distinct feeling that he didn't like me very much. Thankfully John jumped in to save the day and prevent any awkwardness as he got a conversation started again.

The worst part of it all was that, despite the fact I found Rob rude and obnoxious, and despite the fact I had sworn off men completely, I couldn't help noticing that he was ridiculously attractive. Why was it that all the worst men were blessed with the best looks? How were women supposed to deal with that? Even though I was still angry with him, all through dinner I was very, very aware that he was sat right next to me. I really shouldn't have been noticing that his eyelashes were unfairly longer·than most women who had applied ten coats of mascara, but I was. There was even a couple of times we even clashed elbows. Although touching elbows was hardly scandalous, erotic fiction material, it was pretty much the most action I'd had in a while, even when I had been in a relationship. Something else to stick in the *Jess' Pathetic Life* folder. When Lucy started to clear the plates away, I practically jumped out of my seat to help her, just to get some breathing space.

"So you putting Rob in his place was a highlight of the evening," she said with a smile once we were safely in the kitchen.

"I'm sorry about that," I replied, feeling my cheeks burn with embarrassment again at my out of character outburst.

"Don't be. He needed that. But apart from him being a bit of an arse, what do you think of him?"

"That he's a bit of an arse," I said with trepidation, attempting to make a joke. Thankfully Lucy laughed, not worried I was insulting her brother at all. "I'm sure he dislikes me and I haven't even had a chance to do anything wrong yet. Do you know why he might hate me?"

"Oh that," she replied with a casual wave of her hand, "yeah, just ignore it. He's not great around women. He's much more comfortable in the company of just men."

"Really? Ok. I wouldn't have thought that when I first met him and my gaydar is normally really good. I knew my friend Rich was gay before he even really knew it himself. Was it a big surprise for you when you found out?"

Lucy stared blankly at me for a second and I wondered if I had it all wrong for a second. "I was really surprised when I was first told about it actually. Would you mind carrying this through for me? Thanks," she added in an unnaturally quick tone as she changed the subject and handed me a giant glass bowl filled with tiramisu. It was a fair turnaround though, since I had been quite nosy about what could be a sensitive subject for her family.

As I walked back into the dining room, I felt more comfortable about sitting back down at the table now I knew all the elbow-related sexual tension had been in my head. At least Rob being gay sorted one of my problems out for me.

Chapter 6

"Guess what?"

Lucy bounded back to the table as I stabbed my thumb for the millionth time. It was only our third sewing bee but Ashley and Lucy were already playing about with their machines for this week's cushion project whereas I was not allowed anywhere near a needle attached to a motor until I had mastered the art of not hurting myself with one in my hand. At my current level, if I was going to get behind the pedal of sewing machine, I was likely to massacre everyone in the room.

"Elastoplast are going to start sponsoring my sewing sessions?" I asked as I sucked my thumb to clear away the spot of blood.

"I've finally sorted out my private sewing lessons with your gran. We're going to do four days a week," she beamed. "She says I show natural talent."

"We could have told you that," Ashley chipped in from behind her machine.

"That's only the tip of the good news iceberg. Jess, I just got a text from Rob saying that if you want that waitressing job, you can have it. He suggested popping in on Sunday, about eleven, for an informal interview and to get the lay of the land, so you can decide if you want to work there or not."

I imagined Lucy had used a lot of creative license on Rob's text. I couldn't imagine Mr Grumpy asking me to "pop in" and decide if I'd like the job or not. He'd probably shoved some expletives in there as well.

But I did need a job, and soon, despite what Gran thought

"Tell him great." I forced a smile. "And thank you. I'll be there on Sunday."

She waved her hand away dismissively. "Think nothing of it. Besides, it's your choice if you want the job; I've already told him to hire you and I have a very big say in that place."

"You do? Ow!" Apparently I couldn't talk and sew at the same time.

"I invested in the restaurant because...because it was a good opportunity." Her smile seemed a little over bright and I knew she was on the verge of saying something else, but I was hardly going to pester her for information. "But if I tell him to hire you, then he has to."

"You own a stake in his business and you want to start your own up? You're quite the little entrepreneur," Ashley smiled before her head disappeared back behind the sewing machine

"Well they did approach me to head up *The Apprentice* but I had to turn them down because I was much too busy and they went with some nobody called Sugar in the end."

"I don't think I can picture you firing people to be honest." Though I could picture her brother doing it, not that I was about to say that out loud. While that Daniel definitely deserved to be sacked, I had the impression Rob might have enjoyed doing it.

By the end of the evening, both Lucy and Ashley had sewn the covers for their cushions and stuffed said covers with a couple of white, square cushions Gran had picked up for us to use. Obviously, I hadn't even made a start on mine yet.

After everyone had slowly trickled out, much later than the official session end time of 9pm as there was leftover cake that needed eating and more gossip that still needed trading, I made a start on clearing up the scattering of fabrics and spools of thread still scattered on the table.

"Don't worry about clearing that just yet Jess. Can you sit down for a minute; I need to talk to you about something."

I dropped a pair of fabric scissors into the special Sewing Bee box and followed Gran over to the sofa, where she took a seat and patted the space next to her.

"Everything ok Gran?"

With everything that had happened recently, I should have been making more of an effort to make sure she was ok. Sure, she had seemed fine on the outside but I needed to be looking closer since she was very much from the Stiff Upper Lip generation.

"Yes, fine darling. I just wanted to give you this."

She handed me a piece of folded paper which when I unfolded it, I realised was a cheque and when I read it properly, I felt my stomach leap.

"Gran, I think you put the decimal point in the wrong place. This can't be right."

Surprisingly, my grandmother just laughed. "I haven't quite gone batty yet. That's the right amount. The money for your grandfather's life insurance came through this morning and since my pension covers my outgoings and we already had savings, there was no point me just letting this sit in the bank getting dusty. It makes more sense to give half to you and half to your parents. You'll get it when I'm dead anyway, so I might as well get the chance to see you enjoy it."

"Gran! Please don't say things like that. Are you sure everything is alright?" I'd just lost my grandad; I don't think I could cope if Gran wasn't well.

"Sorry darling." She obviously sensed my distress and began to smooth my hair away from my face. "I didn't mean it like that but I'm just being practical. I meant what I said about seeing you enjoy it. In fact, that's my only stipulation for the money. I don't want you to use it on something sensible, I want you to use it for something for yourself that will make you happy. Anything as crazy as an exotic trip to Timbuktu to treating yourself to a Birkin bag, it's yours to use recklessly. If you buy Premium Bonds with it, I'll know and I won't be best pleased."

I looked down at the slip of paper again and my eyes welled up with tears. "But probability wise, it would be a sound investment," I joked weakly.

"Jessica Mary Crawford!" she said as she playfully swatted at my arm. "Don't you dare even think about anything so sensible. And I'll also know if you refuse to cash it."

That was probably true. She was too perceptive for her own good and I had the feeling that if I didn't cash it within the next couple of days, she would probably march me down to the bank herself. "Ok. I'm still not entirely pleased with this as it's way too generous, but I promise I will cash it."

I had no idea what I would spend it on. Maybe I could take a big trip; it had been a long time since I'd had a holiday and my Uni days had been filled with ideas for travel. But given my current life position, I wondered if I could keep it for something else. Maybe a house deposit. Once I had a full-time job again, I could start looking at getting my own place. I was starting to build some kind of life in Pickney and house prices were very reasonable, so that would be a good option.

"Something fun and a little reckless," Gran's reminded me. "I know that look. Trust me Jess, you need to do these selfish things while you're young. I had a wonderful life with your grandfather, truly I did and I couldn't have asked for a better life, but it's only when you get to my age, you can look back and wonder if you shouldn't have done everything so by-the-books. Everything is so accessible to you these days, so make it worthwhile. Would it make you feel better if I told what your parents are planning to do with their share of the money?"

"Actually, it would."

I adored both my parents and had had a wonderful upbringing but if they were a colour, they would be beige. You could always rely on them to be completely reliable and predictable, never straying from their comfortable routine. I found it difficult to picture them bowing to Gran's whim of doing something adventurous with the money. Dad would probably take out a lifetime membership to the National Trust as opposed to his current annual one.

"They've decided to travel across Asia for a few months," she said simply.

Oh.

"Can you say that again? I thought you'd said they were going to travel around Asia."

Gran gave me a smile that said she was as surprised by their decision as I was. "I'll have to admit, that wasn't the answer I expected but your father said it's something they'd been thinking about for a while. They've found a tour that takes them through a couple of countries over three months. Apparently they were planning to do the one-month tour as a retirement treat anyway, but now they're going to do the longer trip."

Ok. So they had pretty much met Gran's criteria to do something crazy, then completely blew it out the water. If my safe, comfortable parents, who went to the same B&B in Edinburgh every May and the same hotel in the south of France every August, could do something a bit crazy with this gift, maybe I could too.

"I'm still trying to process that my parents are going on some kind of adult gap year."

"You and me both Jess," Gran chuckled. "But don't let on that you know. I think your mother wants to tell you herself once it's all booked and official. Do you have any idea what you want to do with your share?"

Not quite sure how to respond without bursting into tears, I flung my arms around Gran's shoulders. "I promise I'll do something adventurous with the money. But I'm going to give you one last chance to take the cheque back and assuage my guilt."

"All I want for you is to be happy. That's all I need now."

But that was the million-dollar question; what would make me happy these days?

Chapter 7

Since I was still technically unemployed and Gran was refusing to take any contributions to the household bills (not that I had a lot of extra money lying around since I had promised not to use the life insurance money for anything too serious) I was using my days to help more around the house as a way of showing how grateful I was. Cleaning, doing the washing and running errands were all things I was perfectly fine with. I wasn't even that bad at basic DIY. But the one area I couldn't help with was gardening and considering the size and contents of Gran's garden, and with spring almost upon us, that area definitely needed a few extra green fingers.

The garden had been a labour of love for both my grandparents and they had always managed but there was no way Gran could do it on her own. Tending the flowerbeds was fine but I would be neglecting my role of responsible granddaughter if I let her loose with their monster of a lawnmower. After a bit of pestering, I'd finally managed to persuade her to get a gardener in for a couple of days a week to help out.

One of her friends had recommended the guy they used and he was having a trial run today, having turned up mid-morning. I'd been in my room scrolling through job websites and sending out my CV, just in case the waitressing option didn't work out. When I finally appeared downstairs to make myself a late breakfast, Gran was at the table with Lucy.

"You're keen," I commented, looking at the pile of fabric strewn across the wooden surface.

"It's not like I'm doing much else with myself these days," she shrugged. "I might as well dive right into it."

I knocked the kettle on and offered to make a round of tea. If Lucy was going to be here for most of the day, she would definitely need it.

"Jess, I forgot to offer the young man doing the garden a cup of tea. Would you mind going to see if he'd like one?"

Like most people of her generation, Gran probably considered it a cardinal sin that she hadn't offered him tea and biscuits as soon as he had walked through the door.

"And take out a pack of those chocolate digestives," she added as I was slipping on the shoes I kept by the back door.

Right on cue, I thought as I smiled to myself and grabbed the biscuits.

I headed straight for the figure giving one of the rose bushes a haircut, chocolate covered sustenance in hand. "Hi."

I was fully prepared to extend my one-syllable greeting when the words froze on my tongue in surprise. The gardener turned around and he was definitely not what I expected. Two shockingly green eyes met mine, along with the brightest smile I had probably ever seen. A smile so wide, it revealed two deep dimples in the young face. I'm not sure why, but I had been expecting someone older than the gardener in front of me, who was probably about my age, even though Gran had used the phrase *young man*. But, in my defence, she referred to anyone under the age of fifty like that.

"Hey, I'm Riley," he said with a more casual inflection to his words, hinting that his accent wasn't entirely British.

He took off one of his gloves and extended his hand to me. I wasn't able to tear my eyes away from his magnetic ones as I shook his hand, feeling the rough callouses of someone used to working outdoors. "Jess. I'm Elsie's granddaughter. Erm, I was sent out here to see if you wanted tea? And to give you these."

I thrust the packet of biscuits at him, having apparently forgotten how to interact with people properly.

"Yeah, tea would be beaut. Thanks. Strong with one. And thanks for the biscuits." He smiled again, deepening his dimples.

I nodded and turned on my heel to get back to the safety of the kitchen where I could sort my head out. Apparently I was no good at forming coherent sentences when faced with an attractive man these days.

"He's nice, isn't he?"

Gran's words struck me as soon as I closed the door and I suddenly realised what she was about. "Gran! You wily old fox. I just realised what you did."

"I was simply trying to make sure that young man didn't suffer dehydration."

"Yeah and I'm Taylor Swift. Come off it Gran."

"What did she do?" Lucy asked, looking up from her sewing with interest.

"My dear grandmother sent me out there, while I was looking a state I might add, to talk to super-attractive gardener probably in the hope that something might be happen. She does love to interfere with my life."

I was smiling now, seeing the funny side of it but I was surprise to see Lucy's face fall a little. I thought I also saw a flash of annoyance cross her face. "She's trying to set you up with the gardener?"

"Fine. Maybe I'm not as cunning as I used to be but I thought, since he's an incredibly handsome young man, there would be no harm in Jess talking to him. What did you think?" she asked me eagerly, now all the cards were on the table.

"I'll admit it, he's pretty hot. But you couldn't have pre-warned me and given me the chance to put a bit of make-up on or at least a jumper without holes in it?"

"Nonsense Jess, you look as beautiful as always. Does he want a tea then?"

"Strong with one," I replied so she could make him his tea.

While she busied herself with the kettle, I sat down next to Lucy and her pile of fabric. "How's the sewing lesson going?"

"Good, I think. Your gran is explaining patterns to me and she's even sharing the secrets of her old pattern book with me," Lucy replied, gesturing at a heavy brown book on the table that literally seemed to be bursting with pages.

"Like stripes and polka dots?" I asked, wondering why someone needed a book that size for those.

"No, sewing patterns. They're like stencils and instructions for making clothes." She pulled the book closer and opened it at a random page to show me what she meant. There was a large sheet of paper that had been folded to fit in the book but when Lucy unfurled it, it seemed be drawings of sections of a skirt. "You follow the pattern set out here, following the measurement formula for what size you need, and when you sew all the pieces together, it should make a skirt."

I flicked through a couple more pages of the book, realising that sewing was a lot more technical than I had given it credit for. Some of this looked akin to rocket science. And I had only just managed to do a line of backstitch without stabbing myself.

"It looks like I'm just going to be using Tuesday nights to eat cake," I laughed as I closed the book and slid it back across the table.

"You're not that bad," Lucy said in that way only a proper friend would, because we both knew I was shocking.

"You're right, I'm not that bad - I'm that awful."

"Yeah, you're not going to win any sewing awards any time soon," she admitted with a smile. "At least you still have your looks though."

I laughed as I picked up a piece of loose fabric from the table and threw it at her own perfectly symmetrical face.

"The tea's ready Jess," Gran called and I pushed myself out of my seat.

"Are you interested in the gardener?" Lucy asked without any preamble, which made me laugh.

"Luce, I've known him all of five minutes. He might be nice to look at but, at the moment, I am completely staying away from men and any kind of relationship until I can sort my own life out."

"Oh that's ok then. Have fun just looking."

I was still trying to fathom her weird remark as I handed Riley his mug. He certainly was nice to look at.

"Thanks. Do you live here too, or are you just visiting?" he asked conversationally.

"Actually, I'm living here at the moment. My life is kind of in a transitional period." My own ears picked up on the embarrassed note in my voice.

He laughed, but not in a way that he was making fun of me. "I wouldn't worry about it. My life is one big transitional period."

"Really?"

"Oh sure. No idea what I'm doing tomorrow let alone five years' time. Never had any clue what I wanted to be or do either. The only thing I am is restless, which is why I'm out here."

"But doesn't that make you feel a bit nervous? Not having plan?" It certainly did me.

"Not at all. If I had to go through life knowing that my tomorrow would be exactly the same as my today, I'd go crazy. I'm already getting restless after doing this gardening work for a month."

"You're not going to stick it out?"

"Nah. That was never the plan. It's my uncle's business, so that's how I got the job. Nepotism at its finest. My parents are back in Oz, but since my mum was English, I can have a British passport. I'm using this time to earn a bit of cash before blowing it all as I work my way through Europe over the summer. I can get around so much easier with a British passport than an Aussie one, which will let me go wherever the wind takes me."

"So you're one of these nomads then?"

"Nomad, gypsy, hobo. Whatever sounds more poetic," he said with the dimpled-smile again.

"Where are you going to go to?"

I set myself down on the grass next to the flowerbeds he was working on and listened to him reel off all the places he wanted to see. It turned out he had no idea where he was going to stay when he got there or even how he was going to get there, only that he was going to go there. The idea of not having much of a plan made me nervous for him but I could already tell that Riley was one of those people who didn't need a plan.

I was also jealous. Not so much for what he was doing but how he talked about it. His face completely lit up and his voice so passionate when he talked about surfing in Portugal or biking through Amsterdam. I couldn't think of anything I could talk about where I would sound so passionate.

"You ever thought of just upping sticks and going somewhere else while you're in your transitional period?" Riley asked as he took his gloves off again and offered the pack of biscuits to me before helping himself to one.

"It's crossed my mind a couple of times," I admitted. "But it's not really me. Maybe a few years ago but I think I'm past all that now."

"Nah, that's the beauty of it, you'll never be too old. You should go and put yourself out into the world."

"I'll think about it," I said as I stood up and brushed the grass of my jeans. "I'll let you get on with your job, but it was nice talking to you."

"You too Jess," he said with that wide smile as he handed me his empty mug.

All this talk of travel made me want to call my parents to see if they were ready to reveal their big surprise yet. Once I was back in the house, I grabbed the phone and settled myself in the living room. I hit number one on speed dial and hoped they were home. The phone picked up on the third ring.

"Hey Mum, just me."

"Jess! Sweetheart. How are you? How's Elsie?"

Bless my mother. She was always so happy to hear from me.

"I'm good and so is Gran. Just thought I'd give you a ring and see how things are." And for you to finally tell me about this big adventure you'd been keeping secret. "It's been almost a week since we last spoke, so anything new going on with you or dad?"

"Actually Jess, we do have a bit of news."

Yes. *Finally.*

"I spoke to your Auntie Lynn yesterday and apparently Rachel is pregnant again. Isn't that wonderful?"

Big whoop. Not that I wasn't happy for her, but my cousin Rachel already had four kids. She'd essentially been continuously pregnant for the last five years, so it wasn't exactly the exciting news I'd been waiting on.

"That's nice. So that's it? Nothing else going on?"

My mother said no but then I heard Dad's muffled voice down the line as he said something to Mum. "Yes there is! I can't believe I forgot all about it. We literally got back from the travel agents half an hour ago. We're going on a trip."

"Really? Where?" I asked, feigning ignorance.

"You'll never believe this but we're doing a three-month trip around Asia. Now where did I put that itinerary?" I heard the echo of papers being shuffled then a silent pause as I pictured my mother putting on her reading glasses. "Here we are. Now, we start in India and spend three weeks going to the northern areas before going to Nepal and we do some camping in one of their national parks, which your father is very excited about because we'll supposedly see all kinds of wildlife."

"Camping?" I interrupted.

"Well, not *camping* camping. I think they call it glamping these days. It'll be camping but nicer. After a week there we then go onto Bhutan, Burma, Laos, Vietnam and Cambodia, which is going to take another six weeks to work across. Finally, we finish up in Thailand and we get a whole month there! Doesn't it sound exciting?"

"Sounds amazing Mum." Half of me was tempted to ask if there was room for one more on this trip. "A proper adventure."

My mum's warm laugh trickled down the line. "I suppose it is. Though we're hardly adventurers. We have a guide with us every step of the way and get taken to everything, so there's no risk of us getting lost in the middle of the town whose name we can't pronounce. But it will be exciting."

We talked for a little longer as I filled her in on some of the coming and goings from Pickney. To her immense credit, she never asked when I was going to find myself a job or added any pressure to make me feel bad about it and I greatly appreciated that. I think she could tell that I was already a lot happier than I had been a few weeks before, even if I wasn't quite back to my old self just yet.

Maybe Riley was right and I should put myself out there in the world again. A trip to do that would certainly meet the terms Gran had about spending that money. It seemed everyone was about travel or holidays at the moment. Even Gran and Olive had been discussing the idea of a weekend away somewhere.

But I wasn't convinced it would make me happy in the long run. While it would be nice to get away, I couldn't help feeling that at this point in my life, anywhere I went would just be an excuse to run away from my current problems and help me avoid them for a little bit longer.

Well, I was done running from my problems.

Chapter 8

If I needed any more evidence that Lucy was quickly becoming a great friend, it was the fact she came with me to my "informal interview". When I tried to thank her, she brushed it away saying that she sometimes headed to the restaurant to help her brother out but I knew that she was only heading there to put me at ease.

I'd been feeling slightly nervous, mainly because I had this nagging feeling that Rob really didn't like me, though considering his demeanour, he might just not like anyone full stop.

After parking round the back of the building, I followed Lucy through the back door where it was eerily quiet. She called out to Rob but there was no answer and we both walked through to the main part of the restaurant and found him behind the bar with a clipboard.

"I can do that Rob," Lucy said without any preamble as she went to take the clipboard from him, "so you can show Jess around."

He looked over at me as if only realising I was there and didn't look that pleased to see me. Maybe he had been hoping I wouldn't show. His serious demeanour automatically dissolved my confidence and I offered him an awkward smile instead.

"You'll need to cover all the drinks," he said to his sister. "Don't forget it takes three days for the wine to get delivered so don't leave me short on bottles. Count what we've still got out back."

"How many times have I done this Rob?" Lucy replied with a patient smile. "I know what I'm doing. Stop making Jess wait."

He gave her one last look before heading over to me and I quickly tried to claw some of my confidence back and held my hand out to him. "Thanks for this," I said in what I hoped was a professional tone.

He shook my hand although he looked confused at my gesture. Maybe I should tone down the levels of formality. I now felt that turning up in a blouse and pencil skirt was a bit too much for a Sunday morning looking around an empty restaurant. I probably could have just worn jeans.

"So yeah, this is restaurant. Obviously." He gestured around him and although I had been here once before, I had been more preoccupied with forming new friendships. Now I was able to properly take in the atmosphere. It did look very Italian and it was clear a lot of effort had gone into the decoration. It was simple and created a cosy atmosphere, one that I thought would be even better in the evening with soft lighting and candles on the table.

The restaurant wasn't huge, but the wooden tables had been arranged in a way that still gave people enough space not to feel claustrophobic. The exposed brick walls were decorated with water colours of what I guessed was Italian landscapes and there were odd tokens scattered about the place to enhance the Italian theme. It actually reminded me of a place I'd been to in Florence when I travelled through Italy with a couple of friends after the first year of Uni, which seemed a lifetime ago now.

"There's four wait staff at the moment, five if you take the job, and we generally have regular shifts set out but there's always the option to swap shifts around. Two staff are usually enough at lunch and during the week but Friday and Saturday nights, I like to have three in if I can."

"I can do whenever you want and as many shifts as you need. I'm not fussy," I said quickly, maybe with a little bit too much enthusiasm.

"Good to know. Flexibility would actually help me at the moment. So along with the wait staff, there's a couple of young lads who do the washing up and help prep the food in the kitchen, an assistant chef and I do the bulk of the cooking."

"You do all the cooking *and* run the place?"

"It's because he's too much of a control freak to delegate," Lucy shouted over from the bar.

"We're closed all day Sunday and Monday afternoon," Rob continued, acting as if he hadn't heard her. "Otherwise we open for lunch and close at eleven every day. Final order time for dinner is nine. I usually come in on a Sunday to sort out all the little things and also get prep done for the week. I make all the pasta fresh, so I make it in bulk on a Sunday and we freeze it, but if I need to make it during the week, I still can. In fact, we try and make as much from scratch as we can."

He might act like a grumpy bastard but you certainly had to respect the guy. Owning the business and practically running every aspect himself? He certainly was dedicated.

"There's no official uniform just black trousers or skirt and a white shirt, which you're responsible for providing yourself as I know people can be funny with clothes chosen by someone else." His eyes swept down the length of me and I couldn't help the spike in my body temperature. "What you're wearing now is fine actually."

"Black and white, got it."

"So, the bar is over there," he said dismissively. "If it's not busy, someone will usually take over bar duty and make up the drinks so you won't have to do it, but if it's an all hands-on deck kind of night, you might have to sort out your own drinks orders."

"That's fine. I've done bar work before, so I know what I'm doing."

He nodded. I took his silence as the fact I had said something that pleased him. "Wine's pretty important here and I get a lot of it sent over from Italy, so we'll need to cover the best types to have with different foods if you don't already know. And I'll give you a crash course with the coffee machine since we do the proper stuff here, not that instant shit."

"No, if course not," I said, not knowing how else to reply. I didn't mind instant coffee; it did its job as far as I was concerned.

"Sorry," he said, dialling down his brusque manner. "It's an Italian thing. We're very picky with coffee. I'll show you the kitchen."

I followed him through double swing doors into the pristine kitchen that was a lot bigger than I expected it to be. "What's that over there?"

"Wood oven for the pizzas. We make them all fresh and cook to order but they only take eight minutes in the wood oven. So, that's the general overview, what else do you need to know? Right, money. It's minimum wage but sometimes since shifts are covered at short notice for whatever reason, I'll up it to time and a half to say thanks."

"That's really nice of you," I said, voicing my surprise out loud but he continued talking as if he hadn't heard me.

"All tips you earn are yours. I've told you what hours we operate and I can try to get you in a regular kind of shift pattern, but like I said before, I'd appreciate whatever you can do at the moment while I re-sort things out. And I know this is only a temp job to do us both a favour but if I could get at least a weeks' notice when you decided to move on, that would be helpful."

"Yeah of course. And like I mentioned, I can basically do as many shifts as you'd need me for. I'm really not fussy at the moment. Though if I can keep Tuesday nights free, that would be great as that's the night we have our sewing bee."

He tilted his head to look at me properly before nodding. "Shouldn't be a problem. Can I get your decision by the end of today?"

Before I could answer, Lucy's smiling head popped through the kitchen door. "Everything going ok in here?"

"Have you finished with the drink levels?" Rob asked in an obviously annoyed voice.

"Almost, just taking a little break," she beamed as she walked into the kitchen and over to us. But she then caught me completely off guard when she addressed her brother in, what I assumed was, flawless Italian. Rob then responded in equally, again what I assumed was, flawless Italian. Considering it was their heritage, I shouldn't have been surprised by their bilingual talents but hearing it was something else.

Though I had no idea what was going on, the annoyed noises coming from Rob and his exaggerated eye rolls were enough to tell me that he wasn't really enjoying whatever Lucy had to say. But she didn't seem to be relenting and the tempo soon picked up.

My head swung between the two of them as I watched the verbal tennis match going on. The both fired out their lightning fast Italian and I was sure that even if I understood some of the language, I wouldn't have been able to pick any of it up at this pace. They were even gesturing with their hands in the way I was led to believe Italians did when they were talking. Both voices were getting louder and faster, but Lucy didn't seem to be getting quite as worked up as Rob.

"Lucia," he said finally in what even I knew was a warning tone, "*basta!*"

Wait. Had he just called his sister a bastard? Probably not, since Lucy didn't look offended in the slightest. Instead, she just smiled sweetly at him and replied, "*Va bene, Roberto, va bene*," before giving him a little wave and walking out of the kitchen.

Rob muttered a few words under his breath that I was almost certain this time were actually swear words and for some reason I thought it would be a good idea to pipe up because it might ease the tension.

"You speak the lingo too? That's really impressive." I wasn't even being sarcastic. I was always impressed by bilingual people because I was so rubbish with languages. I had only just managed to scrape a C in GCSE French, not helped at all by what my teacher described as a "*terrible and quite insulting French accent*". What had made that grade look even worse was the fact my own mother was self-taught fluent in

French and had made a career out of translation work but apparently I had not inherited the language gene.

"Not that impressive. It helps when people speak it to you as you grow up." He shrugged as it if was nothing at all, now the tension had dissolved. "I just picked it up without having to do anything."

"Did you grow up in the UK or Italy?"

"UK. But my grandparents on my dad's side didn't speak English so we needed to know Italian or it would have been really awkward during our visits with them. Actually, my mum's parents preferred to speak Italian to us even though they lived here and spoke English perfectly. I guess it was a preservation of heritage or something."

"Was your mum born here then?" I asked, aware that I was now bombarding him with personal questions, but all this stuff fascinated me. Until my dad moved to Oxfordshire for work just before I was born, all known family history, on both sides, was contained within a twenty-mile radius of Pickney. That was as exotic as my family got. Though mum had au paired in Paris when she was younger, which upped the exoticness a little.

"Yeah. My grandad was a professor who specialised in Roman History and ended up working in London after being poached from Sapienza. Rome's university," he added quickly, obviously realising I didn't know where or what Sapienza was. "Mum was born here but actually went to Sapienza for Uni herself, which is how she met Dad. After living in a few different countries because of work, they settled here. So that's basically my family history for you."

It was strange but once I got talking to Rob, I felt more comfortable than I expected. He wasn't being as grumpy as he usually was. In fact, when he talked about his family, his handsome features softened and made him even more attractive. Just because he was gay didn't mean I couldn't appreciate the view.

"So why cooking? It sounds like your family were quite the academics."

He actually laughed, which I think was the first time I had heard him do so. Granted, I'd only met him once before, but that night had included John and Ryan and they were hilarious when they were together.

"Not my paternal grandparents; they were very food orientated. Nonno Lorenzo owned a bakery in the small town they were from and my nonna just loved cooking. Lucy and I would spend whole summers with them and they taught me everything I know."

"There are worse ways to learn. It sounds so picture perfect."

"It really was," Rob replied, his face practically shining with happy memories. "It was all hot summers, cobbled streets, fresh focaccia, pasta and olive oil on everything. My grandparents were those typical Italians. Passionate about everything, very family orientated and devout Catholics. They loved tradition."

"Were they supportive of you when…" I trailed off, mentally kicking myself for speaking without thinking.

"When I what?"

"No, it's nothing. Absolutely none of my business." Our nice chat had somehow made me think for a split-second that we were friends and I had an all-access-pass into his private life.

Rob's brow furrowed slightly and although he wasn't looking like he had the first night I met him, he wasn't exactly Mr Happy now. "Obviously it was something or you wouldn't have started to ask. Come on."

"Well, it's just I heard it's difficult to come out to older relatives who are stuck in their ways, especially religious ones. One of my friends from home had that problem with his grandma and it really upset him."

"You think I'm gay?"

Oh no. So much for making that good impression. I'd unintentionally gone and offended my potential new boss. A man who didn't seem to like me as it was. And we had started to get on so well.

"Erm, yeah. But it's fine. I definitely don't have a problem with it. Not that there's a problem to have anyway."

Shut up, shut up, shut up. I needed to stop myself babbling before I dug myself into an even bigger whole and got myself sacked before I even started.

But funnily enough, Rob didn't seem that angry. He crossed his arms and leaned back against the worktop, scrutinising me. "What brought you to this conclusion then?"

The hole I was in was now so deep, I could barely see daylight, so I might as well be honest. It's not like I could make things any worse. "Lucy mentioned it. She was talking about how you had a problem being around women and were much more comfortable around men. I didn't mean to pry into your personal business, but I was a bit surprised, which is what made me make a comment to Lucy. She said she was just as surprised when she found out too."

I watched as Rob's face changed and realised I could actually make things worse. His mouth fell back into the stern line I was so used to seeing and he straightened up and strode out of the kitchen.

I wasn't exactly sure how I could fix this, but I definitely needed to apologise, so I hurried out after him. He was already at the bar, glaring down at Lucy who was checking the wine levels.

"Luce, do you want to tell me why you've been telling your friends that I'm gay?"

Lucy stood up and met her brother head on. The look on his face was rather frightening, but Lucy stayed her ground and almost looked like she was going to laugh.

"I never said you were. I just never completely denied the wrong conclusion Jess came to. But look at it this way, it gave the two of you something to talk about."

My head was starting to hurt from where all of this was going. Where was all this going? Although as I replayed the conversation with her in my head, I realised she hadn't actually confirmed or denied anything in so many words. She just let me go on thinking what I thought.

"But you said he has a problem being around women," I blurted out to Lucy.

"He does," she replied before her brother could argue. "Well, not women in general – he's not a misogynist or anything. Basically, he only has a problem with one woman, but he's letting her affect his perception of all women. He just needs someone to show him that all women aren't the same."

"Lucy," Rob said with a clear edge to his voice, "keep out of my business. Stop discussing personal things with just anyone. And you," he pointed over at me, "take the job, don't take the job. I really don't care. If you are taking it, your first shift will be tomorrow, be here by half four. Now I'm going to deal with a load of paperwork I have clogging up my desk so I don't have time for any more childish games."

As he stormed off into the manager's office, I tried to work out what happened. Had I started all of this somehow? And did I really want to work with someone who seemed like such a time-bomb?

"Don't worry about him," I heard Lucy say. "He just gets a little over sensitive at times. I've tried being nice, but I think I've reached the point where only tough love is going to work now."

As much as Rob had already demanded that Lucy stay out of his business, I was still curious to know what was going on. I might be working for the man after all. "What really happened?"

Lucy walked around to the other side of the bar and hopped up onto one of the stools, patting the one next to her for me to sit down too.

"He hasn't always been this serious. And if you catch him at the right time, he really can be a lot of fun. But, as with most stories like this, it all starts with a woman."

"Are you sure it's ok for you to tell me this?"

She stared at me for a second with her warm eyes that were so like her brothers, before smiling. "I think if anyone should know, it's probably you. So, a couple of years ago, he was with a girl called Sally. I don't know why, but I couldn't make myself like her. Rob was head over heels in love with her though and he was happy, which was all that really mattered. I think she loved him too, in her own way, but she was too selfish to really love anyone properly, apart from herself of course."

This was definitely heading into personal territory that I had no right to be in. At the same time, I wanted to know more. For whatever reason, I wanted to know about Rob and why he was like he was.

"So I guess the relationship ended quite badly?" I asked.

Lucy nodded. "She put him through hell first though. He had just opened this place and everything was going so well. She was helping him run it, overseeing everything out the front. It took a couple of months for him to work it out, but he found the books weren't adding up. He thought it might have just been his maths, so he got me to go over them and I was able to spot it instantly. Someone was ciphering funds from the takings."

"Sally?"

I don't even know why I asked. I already knew that was the answer.

"Yep. It was a classic kind of case. She started off so small that no one could really notice anything but after a couple of months without getting caught, I guess she got greedy and upped her game. That's how you get caught. That's how they always get caught."

"What did Rob do?"

Somehow I couldn't picture Rob handing her over the police. I didn't even know him that well, but for some reason, I just knew that he wasn't that sort of person.

"Confronted her, obviously. He was more than hurt but he wanted to understand. It turned out she had a gambling problem no one was aware of but she had gotten herself in quite deep, owing money to a lot of people. That was when he did the stupidest and most reckless thing he's ever done. He paid off all her debts."

"What? From his own money?"

Lucy's pretty face contorted, showing just how much this all still affected her. "It took all his savings. I tried to talk him out of it, but he was convinced it was the right thing to do. If he could wipe her slate clean, then they could have a fresh start themselves. He'd made his mind up."

"It all sounds too easy."

With each passing second I was feeling even sorrier for Rob, who I had clearly misjudged. Maybe he was fully justified in being a bit ill-tempered.

"It was far from it though. He didn't know how bad the addiction was. I think she did try for him, but not hard enough. Three months later, she fell off the wagon big time and finally shattered his already fragile heart. She cleaned the safe out and was able to transfer money from the business account, stealing everything she could get her hands on. She took it all and did a runner, leaving only a note saying she was sorry and she hoped he would forgive her one day. That finally did it. He reported her but by the time she was caught, the money was gone. With a lack of funds, he came really close to losing this place, which I think was probably the worst betrayal of all. She knew how hard he had worked for all of this and how much he loved it, but she didn't care if he lost it or not."

"What saved the restaurant?"

"I did. I still had my share of our parents' money and I gave it all to him to be able to keep the restaurant running." She gave me a little smile. "He's been paying me back, with interest. I don't want the interest, but he's nothing if not proud and wanted to make sure I got more than my original investment. That's why now is a good time to try and set my own business up."

Everything was now falling into place. Why Rob and Lucy were so close, why she was the only person he didn't snap at, why he was so closed off. I thought I'd been betrayed by Liam, which I had, but his betrayal wasn't as lasting as this. Yes, he'd broken my heart and damaged my self-esteem, but it finished there. Rob had not only lost the woman he loved, but he almost lost his business, his security and his dignity. The ghost of Sally would still be wandering around his business and he was never going to be able to shake the memories.

As I processed all the information, I made my decision. I was going to take the job.

Chapter 9

Apparently doing work that confined you to a desk, even if it was only temp work, had made me forget how difficult waitressing could be. And I definitely hadn't broken in my new ballet flats well enough because I could already feel the blisters forming just above my heels. Hopefully Gran had plasters at home.

"For your first shift, you did good Jess."

I smiled at Graham's praise, liking him even more than when I had first started my shift. I remembered him as the guy who was a vast improvement over that awful waiter on my first visit to the restaurant. Working with him only confirmed how lovely and laid-back he was.

"Don't worry, it's not usually this hectic on a Monday night," he continued. "We don't normally get a last-minute table of fifteen turn up for a birthday meal."

"At least they tipped well," I grinned, setting down a small pile of notes and coins on the table we had just cleared. "What's the tip protocol here?"

"We normally pool everything from that shift and split it evenly," Graham replied as he pulled out his own tips and added them to mine. "Thank God that party did come in or this pile would look pretty pathetic."

"You split the money while I go bag up the table cloths?"

He nodded as I carried an armful of table clothes and napkins to a small room at the back of the restaurant where the linens were kept. Before my shift, Graham had talked me through the bagging process and how a laundry company picked the bags up every day for washing, but I wanted to give it a go myself.

I double-checked my counting before tying up the bag and writing the totals down on the main ticket. Nice and simple.

Graham had already turned all the chairs onto the tables and was mopping around them. "Mind the floor. And your share of the tips is over there; you definitely earned it."

I scooped the money up and put it back in my apron pocket. This was going straight into the jar I'd taken out of Gran's cupboard and I was determined not to touch the money until I had filled it.

"Kitchen's done and Leo's now leaving. Graham, can you still catch your friends' gig if you leave now?"

I turned as Rob came out of the kitchen and watched the exchange between him and Graham with interest. Even though Rob didn't strike me as the sort of boss to get too chummy with his employees, he did seem to know quite a bit about their personal lives.

"If you don't need me anymore boss man then I can catch the start of their set. Sure you don't want to come?"

"My answer is the same as always," he replied as he moved behind the bar to start cashing up the till. Apparently he always dealt with the money, unless Lucy was in to lend a hand, and I could fully understand why.

"One day mate, one day." Graham grinned that infection grin of his. "How about you Jess? Fancy coming out?"

"To what?"

"My friends' band are playing at The Cube at twelve. Cheap drinks until 2am!" he added, obviously trying to sell the idea to me.

I laughed wondering if I was so out of touch that I'd completely missed Monday becoming the new Friday. Not that I'd had a real Friday night out in a long time.

"Thanks for the offer but if I don't get home before midnight, I turn back into a glass pumpkin."

I was almost positive that I heard a small snort of laughter come from Rob but when I glanced his was, he had his serious face on as he worked through the till receipt.

"Your loss," Graham shrugged as he squeezed the mop out and picked the bucket up. "I'll chuck this and go then. Slaters taters."

"It's student night," Rob said as Graham left.

"Sorry?"

"Monday nights are student nights, which is why there's something on so late," he explained. "Graham's a social butterfly and if he can go out, he will. Just to pre-warn you, he does the occasional lunch shift with a hangover but I've never seen it affect his work."

"Don't worry about me. I'm not really the *go-out-and-get-drunk* kind of girl anymore. I'm more of the *be-in-bed-early-but-if-I'm-feeling-crazy-stay-up-late-and-watch-Netflix* kind of girl these days," I said with a wry smile as I made my own way towards the bar.

"Really?" Rob looked quite surprised and I wasn't sure if I should be insulted or not. Maybe I looked like a party girl? "Well your shift is over now if you want to get home."

"I'll just unload the glasses from the dishwasher so I don't have to do it tomorrow, then that's everything I think?"

I saw Rob nod and we fell into a surprisingly comfortable silence as we both finished up what we were doing. He finished cashing up the till relatively quickly, probably because most customers had paid using card.

"I know you said you like to get home early but do you want to stay for a celebratory drink for getting through your first shift?"

I gawped at him for a second then realised he seemed almost as surprised that he had offered that I was.

"Yeah sure," I said quickly, before he could change his mind. Being a people-pleaser, I was going to make my new boss like me, even if it killed me.

"Ok. Er…just let me stick this stuff in the safe and I'll be back."

He walked away and I was still in a momentary state of shock. Obviously I hadn't mucked up my first shift if he was offering me a drink. And he might not hate me as much as I thought he did after all.

I was putting the last of the clean wine glasses on the shelf when he came back and took two room temperature ones from the back before pulling a bottle out of the wine rack.

"Wine ok?" he asked.

"Just a small glass please. I'm driving back."

He uncorked the bottle of red he had picked out and poured a large drop into the glass before handing it to me. "Try it first. This is the good stuff and I don't want to waste it."

I thought for a second that he was having another one of those digs but I realised he was only joking. Or maybe half-joking because I wasn't sure if he was capable of making a fully formed joke.

Tipping the glass at my lips, I took a sip of wine and immediately tasted something quite bitter, but not in an unpleasant way. It was a lot sharper than I was used to as well, but then again, I never really knew what

I was doing when I was drinking wine. I had usually just, well, drunk it.

"Take another sip," Rob encouraged and I did. This time it didn't seem quite as sharp. "It takes a little time for the palate to get used to all the flavours but it's worth it."

I think he was right and he certainly seemed to know what he was talking about, so I held my glass out for him to pour a proper amount into it.

"That is a proper Tuscan Cabernet wine and you won't find better. Don't listen to the French, they don't know what they're doing. Good wine comes from Tuscany."

"You seem awfully proud of this wine. Did you grow the grapes yourself or something?"

"Not quite." He smiled and it caught me off-guard. Obviously it was just because it was such a rare occurrence. "The vineyard this comes from is run by a family who were friends with my grandparents but I'm not biased when I say how great their wine is. But since I'm such a great supporter of theirs, I do get excellent mates rates."

We fell into that strangely comfortable silence again as I sipped at my authentic and delicious Italian wine.

"Can I ask you a question?"

I looked up from my wine glass and over to Rob, surprised he was keeping this dialogue going and hadn't told me to get out yet. "Yeah sure. I mean, I was pretty nosy about your sexual orientation so I think you're allowed one personal question."

It looked as if he was almost on the verge of smiling so I guessed we'd put that whole incident behind us. "What are you doing here?"

"What do you mean?"

"Here." He gestured in the space around him. "In Pickney. Working as a waitress. What happened to bring you here when you were working in London? I mean, you come across as a clever woman and you'd been doing that start-up business work before, so I had been wondering."

"Lucy didn't tell you?"

"No. She's not a gossip. Just because she talks about my life doesn't mean she does it with everyone. I don't like her talking about things that have happened with me but I kind of understand why she does it."

As his lips pressed into a thin line, I realised he knew that I knew all about Sally. But the fact Lucy hadn't told him about my situation was kind of warming. My situation was hardly a guarded secret but she was a good enough friend not to talk about it with someone else.

"How soon do you want to get out of here?"

"Ah, so it's one of those stories. Do you need more wine?"

"Not when I have to drive but feel free to save it for me for another time."

So I settled myself against the bar and told Rob my sad story. What felt odd was how easy it was talking to him. It seemed he'd completely forgotten about his dislike for me and I was now talking to a friend, based on the understanding looks he was giving me.

"So there you have it," I finished, as I swirled the last of my wine around in the glass. "My life story. I'm basically a walking doormat and it resulted in me having no job, no savings, no home and no boyfriend."

"But you left him; that took real courage. A lot of people stick around when they shouldn't, hoping the other person will change when they never will."

I guessed he was talking about his situation with Sally and considering what he had said earlier about Lucy talking about his personal life, he probably knew exactly what I was thinking. That explained the fact that in a split-second, his face went blank and he stepped into responsible employer mode again.

"You better head home since your shift finished ten minutes ago. You had a good first night and I know this is just a stepping stone until you find something more permanent but you're doing me a favour too, so thank you."

"You're welcome."

And as if he realised he was being too nice again, he gave me a curt nod and said goodnight as he walked to the back office. Working for Rob was definitely going to keep me on my toes. I just didn't understand why he was so reluctant to show what was clearly a nice side lurking underneath the surface, especially with me.

Chapter 10

It had been a couple of months since my big move from London to Pickney and the strangest thing was, when I looked back, it seemed like I had been here for years. In a good way. I had just fallen into a comfortable routine and for the first time in a long time, I felt genuinely content with my day to day routine.

Despite it only being a temporary job, I was really enjoying working at the restaurant. In fact, I was enjoying it so much I had actually forgotten to check the job websites on a regular basis. I'd now had a chance to work a shift with all the other wait staff and I don't think I'd ever met nicer people in my life. Graham was always good fun to work with and I tried to match my shifts up with his whenever I could, which was quite easy as he was doing this full time too. Also on the staff was a lovely woman called Tina who normally did lunch shifts as she had a four-year-old daughter and two students called Joe and Gethin who work their shifts around their college classes. I was even getting on quite well with Rob.

But as great as the people were at the restaurant, the best thing was actually getting paid a decent, steady wage. I had leftover money, something that had not happened since my job in Oxford. With my willingness to work any shift going, even the last minute ones, and not having anything to spend my money on, I actually had savings again.

Gran was still refusing to take any money off me for rent but I was able to find creative ways to get around this. I would sneak out to the supermarket and do the weekly shop, pay for it with my money and have it all in the cupboard before she could realise. She would huff in exasperation but there was nothing she could do about it.

Another great idea I came up with was heading to her hairdressers the day before she had an appointment and paying in advance for her, knowing full well that she might be annoyed when she found out but she wasn't going to make a fuss in a public place about it. Though eventually she stopped telling me when she had an appointment and I would have to sneak a look at her pocket diary to see when her next hair appointment was.

But the best one I came up with so far was also the simplest. If I happened to be in town and browsing, I would try and pick Gran up a little something to say that I appreciated everything she was doing for me, even if she wouldn't let me pay rent. The best one I came across was a replica of the original Roman Holiday film poster. I bought it, along with a frame, and gave it to her. She was so touched by it, she actually forgot to admonish me for spending money on her and hung it in the living room.

Work wasn't the only thing going well. I actually had a social life again and Tuesday nights were easily the highlight of my week. While it was true that I still couldn't sew my way out of a paper bag, it wasn't about the sewing for me anymore. I enjoyed being around the people. I enjoyed Olive's random wittering and cakes. I enjoyed seeing Gran so happy and having something to take her mind off Grandad, even if it was only for a short time. And I enjoyed being around Ashley and Lucy. It seemed fate had played a massive role in our meeting and our lives were already changing because of it. Lucy had a chance to follow her dreams, Ashley was gaining the confidence she needed for motherhood and I had friends, and technically a job, out of all of this.

If I didn't see the girls at the sewing bee, then we would either arrange to do something on a night when I wasn't working or I would randomly run into them in the house since Elsie Crawford's Skills School practically had an open door policy. Lucy was usually here four days a week for sewing and Ashley would come over on one of the other days for a cooking lesson. Though, at some point, the system had gone out of the window and Lucy would be sewing at the kitchen table while Ashley would be learning how to make Yorkshire puddings. This kind of day was the best if I wasn't working because we would then all sit around and eat whatever Ashley had made. Well, that was until Ryan had jokingly complained that she wasn't bringing anything home for him to try.

Always the problem solver, I came up with the idea that Ash just make double the amount and that way we all stayed happy.

It seemed Ashley's original fears of not being about to do *motherly* things was completely unfounded, as proven when she turned up to the latest sewing bee with a batch of fruit scones she'd made that afternoon at home, completely unsupervised, and Dorothy declared them the best she'd had in years.

Lucy had messaged to say she wasn't well and couldn't make tonight's sewing bee so as it was just five of us, we formed one big circle in the living room which gave me and Ashley a chance to join in the gossip. During the first hour, we learned all about Dorothy's granddaughter's recent ballet exam and how Olive's youngest son was planning on moving his family to New Zealand but she couldn't understand why because they weren't going to be able to get decent tea anywhere other than the UK apparently.

"But my Jim says all our children are old enough to know best now. Apparently Tony can earn more money being a doctor over there and have better working hours, so I can see Jim's point I suppose. Almost fifty years we've been together and he's never been wrong about anything important yet. He made my hair go grey earlier than it should have but we've had a good life; I was one very lucky lady to end up with a good man like Jim."

Instinctively, I glanced over at Gran to see how she was reacting to Olive wax poetic about Jim since it hadn't been that long since she'd lost her own husband. Her smile seemed a little tight, but it was only because I was looking for signs she might be upset so I don't think anyone else would notice. Apart from that, she seemed ok.

"Ashley dear, tell us all about your young man," Olive said, leaning forward with interest. "I've been dying to know for weeks."

"Well, it's not quite the standard story," she replied, her eyes darting slightly at the uncomfortable subject. Even I didn't know that much about Ashley and Ryan's relationship and had never asked. Ashley didn't have the fondest memories of her past generally so whenever we found anything out, it was because she had freely offered the information.

"Those are the best kind," Dorothy said warmly. "How long have you been together?"

"I've known him since I was fifteen, he was seventeen at the time, but it wasn't until a few years later that we actually became a couple."

"Ah, young love," Gran stated with a more natural, relaxed smile. "How long have you been married for then?"

"We got married just after I turned twenty, so it'll be ten years this November."

Olive looked suitably impressed as she helped herself to a biscuit on the table in front of her. "Ten years? That's practically a lifetime by the standards these days. You still haven't told us how you met though."

"Well, erm, we both grew up in care and when I was fifteen, I was moved to the same foster house Ryan was living in."

"Oh my goodness. What happened to your parents?"

I thought Olive had finally crossed the line with her personal questions so I stood up, asking if anyone wanted more tea in an attempt to get them off the subject.

"Thanks Jess, but it's ok," Ashley said softly, realising what I was trying to do. "I should be able to talk about this stuff now. It's not healthy to keep it all locked inside."

As I sat back down, Ashley took a steadying breath before telling her life story to the three older women, all of whom had now put their sewing down and were listening with rapt attention.

"I was taken into care when I was ten because my mother wasn't really fit to be a mother. I spent the next eight years passing through children's homes and foster homes. With the benefit of hindsight, none of these places were particularly bad, even if they weren't particularly great either. Most of the foster homes I ended up in were just people looking to make money and while I got the bare minimum, I wasn't uncared for. I was a lot luckier than so many of the kids out there.

Anyway, I met Ryan when I was sent to live with the Kemps. They were ok, just another family taking in kids for the monthly cheque and they already had five kids living there but I had enough space in the room I shared with two other girls and even though they weren't particularly hands on or attentive as foster parents, we were always fed and had a decent roof over our heads. Ryan was the oldest and only had six more months until he turned eighteen and could get out on his own. Since he'd been doing the foster routine for most of his life and had been in some pretty tough houses, he always tried to look out for the other kids. When I first arrived, he told me how things really worked in the house and if I had any problems, go straight to him."

"He seems like a wonderful man," Dorothy piped up. "Is he very handsome? Was it love at first sight?"

Thankfully Ashley smiled, which helped me relax over the guilt that she had been forced to tell us all of this in the first place.

"I'm not sure about love but it was definitely teenaged infatuation at first sight. It was the first time someone had offered to look out for me; that had never happened before so I think that clouded my judgement slightly. But he was gorgeous. He was already six foot by then and starting to fill out. And he had the most beautiful eyes I'd ever seen, a mix of green and grey, along with this massively infectious smile."

I was sure at least two of the other ladies sighed at the picture Ashley was painting for them.

"Of course, back then, I was this scrawny little girl with wild hair, so I knew he wasn't going to look at me like that. But over the next six months, we talked and shared things about our lives we hadn't spoken to anyone else about. Our backgrounds were very similar and he understood me more than most. We became friends and he helped me to stop dwelling in the past and focus on the future. I would tell him all about how I wanted an important job where people noticed me and I made a lot of money so I could afford all the things I'd always wanted growing up but could never have."

"What happened when he turned eighteen?" Gran asked.

"He left," Ashley shrugged. "I was heartbroken. I'd lost my best friend and the only person in the house I could really talk to. But I understood his need to get away from the reminders of the lifestyle we had to live."

"So he just up and left you?" Olive asked incredulously, apparently forgetting the lonely princess in her tower got her handsome prince in the end.

"Not completely," she replied with a poorly hidden smile. "I thought that was it but a couple of weeks after he'd gone, a letter turned up. Since I didn't have regular access to email and he couldn't afford a computer anyway, he wanted to keep in touch through letters."

Now that piece of information had all the ladies *aww*ing at the romance of it all. Me too, if I was being perfectly honest.

"Nice to know your generation hasn't completely forgotten the art of letter writing," Gran nodded approvingly. "Did you keep his letters?"

"They're all still in a box under my bed."

"How wonderful," Dorothy cried, clapping her hands together. "So what happened for the next couple of years?"

"We kept in touch. He managed to get a manual labour job up north, basically doing anything and everything, and was renting this dingy little flat. It was truly awful," she said with a laugh. "Tiny one-bed above a kebab shop in a really dodgy area. I saved up money from my Saturday job to visit him one weekend and got to experience its awfulness first-hand. But it was his own space and that was priceless.

So we both plodded along until I was eighteen. On the day of my eighteenth birthday, as I left the Kemp house, I saw Ryan outside, leaning against this battered old Fiesta with a suitcase on the backseat that contained everything he owned. He laughed at the surprise on my face before saying, *"right, so where are we heading to?"*."

"He didn't!" This time it was my turn to interrupt Ashley. Although knowing Ryan, I could actually picture him doing something like that.

"He did," Ashley laughed. "I told him I was headed to London to make my fortune, so he put my suitcase with his and drove us there."

"Wow. Ryan is a lot smoother than I gave him credit for. When did you officially get together then?"

"Three days later. We were looking over this dank flat in Bethnal Green, even worse than his previous one, and he pointed out we probably couldn't afford more than one bedroom but since he was madly in love with me, he could cope with that arrangement as long as I was ok with it."

Ashley's story had all of us grinning like idiots. "And of course you were."

"Of course. We took that awful flat and he found work where he could while I took on all kinds of day jobs while going to college at night. God knows how we managed to survive but we did. A couple of years later, it all paid off when I got a job in marketing and Ryan was able to start his furniture business up. By then, I'd been working full-pelt for so long, I didn't know how to slow down, so that's how I stayed until I burnt myself and we moved here."

"Whose choice was it to move here?" Gran asked.

"Ryan picked the area but it was me who said I needed to get out of London. I didn't want to have the baby and go back to working the hours I had been because I'd miss out on all the important bits. Ryan chose the countryside so I could relax and plan ahead in peace. And because we had both always dreamed of a cosy house with a big garden when we were growing up," Ashley finished, resting her hands on her baby bump.

"Oh my dear, what a wonderful story. And you. What an inspiring young woman you are," Olive said, reaching across to pat her hand fondly.

"Me? No, I just -."

"You are Ash," I cut across her. "So you better get used to having that label."

And I truly meant that. Growing up, I'd had two loving parents, a good home and basically anything I wanted. The worst thing that had ever happened to me was a cheating boyfriend. My life had been ridiculously easy. But Ashley and her strength inspired me. I was going to stop being so whiny, toughen up and make something of my life.

But first I needed to call my parents for a long chat. They were flying out to India in less than a week after all, so now seemed a good as time as any to make sure they knew how appreciated they were.

Chapter 11

Lucy had missed three weeks' worth of sewing bees and hadn't been round for a single lesson with Gran, which had us all worried. What worried us even more was neither me nor Ashley had seen her in any other social capacity either as she kept cancelling any plans we made for dinner or a cinema trip. She had gone completely AWOL and I was one cancelled plan away from turning up on her doorstep to see what the heck was going on.

Had we offended her in some way and she didn't want to be out friends anymore? It sounded very Primary school but that was how I was feeling.

Rob had also told me Lucy had been off with him too. I didn't know if this made me feel better because she clearly wasn't just avoiding me and Ashley or if it made the situation worse because she was acting strangely with her brother. Rob had at least seen her but he told me that she didn't seem herself at all.

The tipping point finally came through late Sunday afternoon when Lucy sent a message through on the group chat. I'd barely finished reading the message when the call from Ashley showed up on my phone.

"You've read it right?" she asked before I'd even had the chance to say hello.

"Yep. Something's clearly wrong. We need to go round there."

"Agreed. What kind of friends would we be if we just agreed to this?"

"Terrible friends. Pick you up on the way through in about half an hour? I'm going to call Rob as well to let him know what's happened."

As soon as I hung up with Ashley, I dialled Rob to fill him in on the situation like he'd asked me to.

"Jess?"

"Yeah, sorry, I know you're probably busy sorting things out at the restaurant but you wanted to be kept updated on Luce. Well, she's just messaged us and said she's sorry but she won't be coming to the sewing bee anymore."

"What? But she loves your sewing thing. When she first started I couldn't shut her up about it. Did she give a reason why?"

"No. That's the problem. Me and Ashley are going to go round there now and see what's going on because there's clearly something she hasn't told us."

There was silence on the other end of the line for a few seconds and I was waiting for Rob to tell me to stay out of his family's business but then he completely surprised me. "Can you pick me up on the way past? I'm at the restaurant."

"I can be there in about twenty minutes."

Grabbing my coat and bag, I told Gran I was headed to Lucy's but refrained from telling her the reason why. Gran really liked Lucy and I knew she'd worry as well if I told her there was something wrong. I wanted to know what the full story was until I mentioned it to Gran because I had the feeling I might be needing her the kind of wise advice only grandmothers can dish out.

Rob was waiting outside the restaurant when I pulled up and he jumped into the front seat. He said a quick greeting but otherwise our drive to Ashley's house was silent. Not that I could completely blame him. I could tell that his silence was coming from a contemplative state rather than just rudeness. He was clearly worried about his sister who was the only family he had left after their parents had died in a car accident about seven years ago and they were extremely close. The fact that Rob had no idea what had made her so distant made me more than a little worried.

When we reached Ashley's, I called her to say we were outside and she was straight out the front door, apparently ready and waiting, and we made our way to the small village of Henham, just on the outskirts of Pickney, to get answers from Lucy.

Our odd trio pulled up outside Lucy's house and John opened the door, eyes darting between the three of us.

"Please tell me you're here to see Lucy," he said quietly, as if scared he was going to be overheard.

"So something is wrong. We thought as much when she messaged to say she couldn't come to the sewing bee anymore."

John frowned at Ashley. "She quit the sewing bee? You better come in."

We all shuffled into the hallway, waiting for John to explain more of the situation before we just went barging in. "She's been really off for the last couple of weeks but she's refusing to talk to me about it, which is really unlike her. She keeps saying she's fine but I know she isn't and I don't know what to do."

My heart broke a little for John. He looked so forlorn at the idea the woman he loved was suffering in silence about something but there was nothing he could do about it.

"We'll make her talk," Ashley said confidently. "Now, where is she?"

John pointed us to the living room where Lucy was sat at the table with her laptop. As the four of us filed in, she looked up and her eyes widened. Lucy was displaying an emotion I didn't even think she could feel – fear.

"Wh…what are you all doing here?"

"We're here for answers Luce," Ashley said in the no-nonsense tone she probably used all the time back in London. "You owe us an explanation as to why you've been ignoring us all and why you've suddenly quit the sewing bee. And don't you dare tell me it's because you lost interest."

"I'm not going to have time," she replied in a not so steady voice. "I need to go back work. I'm actually applying for jobs right now."

"What about the vintage shop," I asked in obvious surprise. I knew full well what she thought about the idea of going back to being an accountant.

"I don't want to do that anymore."

"For God's sake Luce, stop lying," John said, his usual laid-back demeanour crumbling as he sat in the chair next to her, grabbing her hands. "You've been dreaming of setting up this shop for years. On our first date, you actually told me that you had this crazy dream that one day, you'd like to make beautiful clothes and sell them. You can't tell me you changed your mind overnight. What's happened?"

"It's not realistic. It won't work!" she blurted out, looking surprised she had admitted it.

"Of course it will babe. If anyone can do it, you can," John said soothingly.

"No, it won't. The bank told me it won't work."

"What do you mean?" Rob finally spoke up, taking a step towards his sister.

Lucy looked up at him, tears filling those big Bambi eyes. "I started putting a business plan together and went for a meeting at the bank to see if I could get a small business loan because I realised I can't just use up all our savings for it. It would be selfish and irresponsible and I don't think it would be enough anyway. The bank turned me down."

"Why did they turn you down? With the current financial upturn, they're actually more encouraging of small businesses than they have been for a while."

"Thanks for rubbing it in Ash," Lucy said harshly with a humourless laugh.

I quickly looked over at Ashley, whose face instantly fell. She hadn't meant it as a dig at all and definitely wasn't trying to make Lucy feel worse. Even though Lucy probably knew that, the outburst was completely out of character. Even Rob was looking at his sister as if he didn't quite recognise her.

"I didn't mean it that way Luce," Ashley replied quickly. "I just -."

"It's fine." Lucy cut her off with a little wave of her hands. "I know you didn't. It was my fault anyway. I tried talking them through my idea and showed them some of the projected figures I'd managed to come up with but apparently my idea "isn't viable" and I'm "not a desirable candidate.""

She added air quotes around the bank's comments for the extra effect and tried to smile it off but it looked like she was in pain more than anything.

I wished there was something I go do, something I could say, to make everything seem better but at that moment, my brain was giving me nothing and it made me feel awful.

"That's ridiculous," Rob said. "How can they not think you would make it work? If I can get a restaurant up and running, then you can do this."

"You had experience in that industry. You knew how everything worked," Lucy shrugged. "Me? I'm going into this blind? I might have experience with figures and spreadsheets but really, what do I know about running my own business? It was a stupid idea."

"Of course it's not," Ashley said, moving forward to put an arm around Lucy. "If none of us acted on stupid ideas, nothing would ever get done. If it's more experience you need, then we'll work on getting you some."

"How?"

Ashley frowned before looking at me beseechingly. So far, I'd been about as helpful as a chocolate teapot. Apart from being the driver, I'd contributed nothing to help my friend.

"Start small and do it online," I suggested. "Get John to set you up a website and you can advertise what you've made and also take customer orders."

It wasn't the best idea I could have come up with, but on short notice, it was something. However, John seemed to think it was a good plan.

"See babe, you can still do something with it. I'll design you the best website and it'll have people flocking to see what you've got. You can't give up on this. Everyone does everything online now anyway."

Lucy gave a little nod but still stayed silent. She wasn't latching onto the idea like John was but I was hardly offended. A small website wasn't what she had planned and I knew she didn't want to take things slowly.

"Are you going to come back to the sewing bee?" I asked. "Why did you want to stop in the first place?"

"I didn't want to be reminded of what I had failed at and since I'm not starting up the business, there's no need to go."

"Of course you do! It was fun, it gave us something to do on a Tuesday night and Gran will be really disappointed if you don't come back." I hoped adding a little bit of emotional blackmail at the end might help make her decision.

"You did love going," John added gently. "You said it was the highlight of the week."

Lucy sighed but more in a resigned way that said she knew was outnumbered here. "You're right. I can't do this Tuesday, but I'll come back for the next one. Apologise to your gran for me, since I'm probably really behind now."

She still wasn't back to being herself but we all seemed to take her agreement as a small victory. Baby steps.

We stayed for another half an hour as John made a round of tea but the conversation was forced and it was obvious Lucy just wanted to be left alone to lick her wounds in private. Eventually it was Rob who said we needed to make a move as he had things to finish at the restaurant. We said our goodbyes and left with the promise from Lucy we'd see her sometime during the week. I made a weak joke about making sure Gran made her famous Victoria sponge for her first sewing bee back but it barely got a smile out of Lucy.

The drive back was more subdued than it had been on the way there, if that was even possible. Even though we'd managed to talk Lucy into coming back to the sewing bee and she said we had made her feel better, we knew we hadn't. Not really.

I dropped Ashley back first and she said she'd call me so we could talk some more about ideas to help Lucy, then ran Rob back to the restaurant.

"Do you think she'll be ok?" I asked him before he climbed out of the car.

The look he gave me didn't fill me with confidence. "Honestly? I'm not sure. I've never seen her like this before. But thanks for trying to help."

I could accept his gratitude if I had actually helped but I had done sod all. I didn't deserve to be called Lucy's friend right now but I was determined to rectify that and come up with something to really help her.

Chapter 12

"Jess, you're very quiet. Is everything ok?"

I looked up from my plate of Shepard's Pie that I hadn't eaten but had simply been moving around with my fork. I'd been so distracted by my own thoughts that I'd actually forgotten I was eating dinner with Gran.

"No, not really," I sighed as I set my fork down. "I'm worried about Lucy."

"In what way? I thought you'd persuaded her to come back to the sewing bee?"

"I did but I can't forget how upset she looked by the idea she can't start up her shop. She's just so...defeated. She wasn't her normal self at all."

Ever since Lucy and Ashley had been thrown into my life, I thought them both indestructible. They made me want to be better, to be more like them. Neither of them accepted no for an answer and I thought Lucy, with her larger than life personality, couldn't be beaten by anything.

It had been a week since she'd dropped the news that she was giving up on the idea of opening her own shop and since then I had been over for dinner, where she'd acted normal. Only she hadn't been normal. As much as she tried to cover it, I could see that she was still upset about having to give up on her dream and

John confirmed as much when I was able to catch him for a quick word when Lucy was in the kitchen.

"I see. Is this why she stopped wanting those private sewing lessons?" I nodded. "Why doesn't she think the shop will work? She's a bright girl and when she told me about her plans, they seemed pretty sound to me."

I had yet to fill Gran in on the full story because I hadn't wanted to tell her how broken Lucy seemed but it had now reached the point where I could use some wise words to help me help my friend. "The bank rejected her proposal for a small business loan because her presentation wasn't strong enough. They said they couldn't see it turning a profit and she told us, when she looked at it again, she had to agree. I'm sure there's a way around it, if she tweaks her plans, but she said she's not willing to risk her savings because she doesn't think it's fair on John when they're starting this life together, even though he completely supports her. She thinks she's dreaming too big."

"Or not big enough."

I looked into Gran's crystal blue eyes that were still as sharp as ever, making me think she could see more than she let on. "What do you mean? Do you have an idea?"

"No, that's not my area of expertise. If only we knew someone with a good business mind and experience in setting up new businesses."

"Ok, ok. Point made." I let out a reluctant laugh at Gran's rarely used sarcastic tone. "I'm not going to lie, I have thought a lot about Lucy's plans and where I could fine tune them. Maybe add a little extra here and there. There's so much potential in what she wants to do. The possibilities of where she can take it are endless."

"Why didn't you tell her that?"

"I didn't want to stick my nose in," I shrugged. "It's none of my business. Literally."

"Could you make it your business?" she asked with a badly disguised smile. "Literally?"

I was on the verge of replying, the obvious answer on the tip of my tongue, when the wheels and cogs started to turn. Wheels and cogs that hadn't moved in years but were now starting to shift despite the rust, dust and cobwebs.

"She needs to think bigger," I said slowly, half to myself.

"You don't get anywhere in life if you're not willing to take risks," Gran said wisely.

"You're right." I stood up, the cogs in my brain whirling so quickly now that they were practically steaming. "Thanks for dinner Gran."

She didn't even try to tell me off for barely touching my food as I raced upstairs and pulled out my laptop and a notepad, furiously scribbling down notes.

Gran was right, Lucy needed to go bigger.

It was well after midnight when I finally stopped. I had pages and pages of scribbled notes and sketches on top of Excel spreadsheets I had thrown together and rough mock-ups, almost breaking Grandad's ancient printer that wasn't used to doing so much work. But even then, I was much too excited to fall asleep and had to use every ounce of self-control not to call Ashley and tell her what was happening. I made myself wait until morning, but as soon as the sun was up, I headed downstairs with all my scraps of paper and had a quick slice of toast.

"Jess? Why are you up so early? I didn't think you were working today," Gran asked as she walked into the kitchen. An early riser herself, I couldn't remember ever being up and awake before she was until now.

"I'm not. I need to go round and see Ashley and show her this."

I handed the folder out to Gran and she flicked through the pages before closing it and smiling at me. "Someone was working hard last night. It looks incredible."

Her praise filled me with warmth and what was even better, I knew that what I'd put together was solid. For the first time in a very long time, I was doing something I was good at and doing something that could potentially make a difference in someone's life.

I waited for another hour before I thought it was a reasonable time to go intrude on Ashley and drove over to her house. Ryan opened the door and greeted me with a smile, leading me into living room where Ashley was sat on the sofa, eating cereal from a bowl she was resting on her baby bump, watching the morning news.

"You look comfortable," I said, trying not to laugh.

"I'm pregnant. Apparently growing a person inside me allows me to slob out here instead of eating breakfast at our table like everyone else," she replied, with a pointed look at her husband.

"You should be taking it easy whenever you get the chance. Do you want some herbal tea? Or that coconut water I bought the other day? I don't think you're drinking enough. I'll bring you both."

As soon as Ryan was out of the room, Ashley let out a sigh. "I don't have the heart to tell him I hate coconut water. I don't care how good it is for you, it tastes awful."

"It's nice he's being hands on."

"A little too hands on. I love him but he's treating me like I'm made of glass now. Since I've found out I'm pregnant, I've been resting up but it's starting to drive me mad. I need to get my hands on something, *anything*, that doesn't use the words stretchmarks, cervix or birthing plan."

I finally let out the laugh I had been holding in as I passed her the folder. "Not once do I mention the word cervix in here."

She began to flick through the folder without saying anything, occasionally stopping at the odd page to read it more thoroughly.

"Not bad Crawford. If I'd have known you back in London and what you could put together, I would have helped you get a ridiculously lucrative yet soul-destroying City job."

"Aww Ash, thanks." I smiled, feeling warmed by her praise at my work.

"But seriously, this is really good. Like *really* good. Why are you showing it to me though?"

"I wanted to get your opinion on it first of all. I know you specialised in marketing but you still know how to do all of this as well. And secondly, if you flick to the very last divider, you'll see where I'm going with this."

She turned to the last few pages and my heart leaped into my throat with both excitement and nervousness. Good things had been happening to me since I moved to Pickney and this could be the best of them all, if everything went to plan.

"I'm obviously not forcing you," I said quickly. "The stuff I wrote down there was just my part and I left the option for you as well, but you can say no. I mean, you have a baby to think about too."

Ashley looked up from the folder, grinning at me. "I'm in!"

"Really?" I resisted the urge to start laughing hysterically as the nerves left my body.

"Yep. It's the perfect idea. Though there's still some stuff in here we need to fine tune and add. Plus, I really like this section you've labelled with a giant question mark; that would be a real winner if we plan it right. You might want to tell Ryan to make some more herbal tea because we're going to be here a while."

Chapter 13

I could hardly contain my excitement and by the looks of it, neither could Ashley. We were both grinning as we approached Lucy who spotted our smiles as she looked up from her sewing and immediately switched from contented to wary.

"Why are you grinning at me like psychos?"

While she had arrived at the sewing bee on time and had got stuck straight into project Gran had set her – an A-line skirt - the usual light she had in her eyes when she was here was still missing. Even the older ladies loudly welcoming her back, saying how much they'd missed her and practically throwing homemade cookies at her hadn't helped. But my plan was about to rectify that. We'd given her half an hour to get settled before the ambush.

Instead of answering her, we both pulled out a chair and Ashley dropped the folder on the table. "We've decided between us that you definitely need to start your own business."

Her eyes looked even sadder, if that was actually possible. Exactly like Bambi's after he couldn't find his mum. "I'd love to girls, you know I would, but it just doesn't seem viable. I went through -."

"Switch your finance brain off for a second and just listen, ok?" I cut in. "In this folder, we have created a solid business plan for you. Between my business knowledge, your accountancy experience and Ashley's marketing prowess, we can make this work on a business level. Throw in the fact you have passion for wanting this to succeed and we're well away."

"But neither of you have the time -."

"Shut up Luce," Ashley interrupted this time. "I'm going to need something to occupy me when I need to get away from nappies and Jess doesn't exactly want to continue serving pizza for the rest of her life. Our proposal is that we invest in this too and do it together."

Lucy didn't even bother saying anything, she just looked from me to Ashley, slightly open-mouthed, so I took the silence as an opportunity to show her the folder. "This is the amount we're both able to invest, so you'd have the majority of the stake in the business with what you have." I flicked through a few pages to the next tab, past some spreadsheets we'd thrown together. "And about your worries that you won't have enough stock to make a profit, we've come up with a solution. Aside from the fact you can make replica vintage dresses like you want to, even taking custom orders, we can also sell genuine vintage items from things we can scout out. Gran's already been in touch with some of her friends and persuaded them to search through their lofts and whatnot for any clothes, shoes and bags from other decades they might have lying around. They've been more than generous because it turns out they'd rather pass them on to someone who might appreciate them instead of waiting for their kids to shove them in a skip once they're dead. We'd be starting out with a good pile of stock that we wouldn't have even spent a penny on so that's pure profit right there."

I paused to take a breath since I'd rattled all of my speech off as fast as possible, partly from excitement and partly to stop Lucy from adding another reason why she couldn't do it. Ashley and I had been through everything with a fine tooth comb and the conclusion we came to was that she really could do this, she just needed a little faith and a lot of courage.

"Ryan also threw in a great idea which I think would really help widen the appeal of the shop. He's been playing about with restoring furniture recently and doing the whole shabby chic thing. He said if he does a few pieces in between his normal stuff, we could put them in the shop. We could either buy the pieces from him and sell them ourselves or we can sell them, he takes the money and we get a percentage as commission. What do you think?"

"Ryan wants to help too? Even though you've got a new born on the way?"

Ashley gave a casual shrug. "He's making the furniture anyway. And I think he's realised how important this idea is to me. We want to help you Luce but we're also being selfish here and doing it for us as well. I might have relaxed a bit but I'm still a complete

Type A and this will give me something non-child related to feed the crazy side of me. And I like to think that as part-owner, you won't have any problems with me bringing the baby to work, so I get to be a mum and work at the same time."

"Well…well of course you could bring the baby. But really, should you be investing in something so uncertain with the baby coming? And Jess, you're only waitressing at the moment."

"I've still got a load of tainted London money to sit on," Ashley replied matter-of-factly. "I don't think you realised how much I was earning before and when you were working thirteen hours a day, you don't really have time to spend it. Plus, houses here are so much cheaper than London so we had some left over from that. Don't worry your pretty little head Lucy Amato, this isn't going to put me and Ryan in the poor house."

"And you don't have to worry about me either." When Gran had given me that money from Grandad's life insurance pay-out, she had made me promise to use it for something important and little crazy. If this wasn't classed as reckless but would make me happy, then what was? "Besides, we're all hoping that it'll pay off in the end anyway. If all three of us invest, you won't need that business loan you were convinced you wouldn't get anyway."

Lucy just continued to stare at us and I wondered if we had her on board or if we'd lost her, so I quickly jumped into another idea we had about trying to hit the public from every possible angle. "And we had this idea of putting in a tea room too as this would probably bring more people in and the profit margins for this would be pretty high because we've got Gran involved in this side. It wouldn't be anything fancy, just tea and cakes, but her friends have volunteered to bake. Most of them do it anyway and they make so much it gets wasted, at least this way...Lucy, are you alright?"

"No," she sobbed, tears suddenly streaming down her face. "This is amazing. You guys are amazing. You didn't have to...I mean, you're not...oh God, I don't even know what I'm trying to say here."

I leaned towards her and I grabbed her hand, giving it a little squeeze. "Say you're on board. Say we can do this."

She nodded frantically as another wave of tears hit and I knew we finally had her. "We can do this. Let's do it!"

And that was the day Deja Vintage was born.

Chapter 14

The change in Lucy was incredible. It was like we had the old Lucy back but then multiplied by ten. I didn't think it was possible for her to get any more radiant but apparently I was wrong.

Our sewing bees had now become planning meetings for Deja Vintage, although Ashley and Lucy were both able to multi-task and sew as we planned. Me? I was just glad of an excuse to spare my poor fingers and offered to take notes instead. It was very safe to say that sewing was definitely not my life's calling.

Unlike Lucy. She was more or less living at our house every day. If she wasn't there for planning purposes, then she was sewing with Gran, who was now supervising her star pupil as she attempted to make her first dress. Like some kind of sewing Yoda, Gran imparted her years of wisdom as she churned out her own designs at a dizzying speed, proving she still had it after all these years. She said since she had the time and all that fabric, she might as well make us some stock for the shop.

I could tell how happy all of this made her and it wasn't just the sewing. She was a major part of the Deja Vintage team and the venture was giving her a renewed purpose, just like it was the rest of us. Plus, I was sure she was on the verge of offering to adopt Lucy and Ashley as her own granddaughters. With Ashley's cooking lessons and Lucy's sewing, she had bonded with them as much as I had.

"You might have to cancel the wedding at this rate," I joked to John over the dinner Lucy had invited me to. "She's basically moved in."

"We'll just have one of those new modern-marriages where we rarely see each other. As long as she still comes back to cook me dinner, I'll be a happy man."

"He'd waste away without me," Lucy laughed as she set a massive dish of food on the table, enforcing her point. "This one has trouble boiling water."

"What's this?" I asked, accepting the second dish which was filled with yellow rectangles.

"Polenta," Rob answered to my right. "Luce will have smothered it in parmesan, just to warn you."

"That's the best way," John said as he leaned over, speared a rectangle and put it straight into his mouth. "I can't even remember my life before polenta. This is the reason I proposed in the first place."

I grinned over at Rob who actually smiled back at me, although it was more of a smile that said his future brother-in-law was a complete idiot. But it was still progress. Following the whole situation with Lucy's employment crisis and the fact I had come up with a solution, Rob had warmed to me considerably. In fact, after my last shift he had actually called me into the office and thanked me for helping Lucy and being, and I quote, *"such a great friend to her"*.

Rob and I were hardly great friends ourselves, by any means, but he had stopped scowling when he looked at me, which was a great improvement, especially since Ashley and Ryan hadn't been able to make this evening's dinner, so it was just four of us. Knowing that Rob might not dislike me anymore certainly made me feel more comfortable being around him with less buffers.

As Lucy served up some amazing lemon and rosemary chicken to go with the polenta, she started filling Rob and John in on all the latest developments in the shop plans and to their credit, neither of them seemed to be showing any outward symptoms of being sick of hearing about it.

"And Ashley started putting together some mock ups of our sign. To keep with the Old Hollywood theme we seem to be veering towards, Jess had the great idea of having it look like the actual Hollywood sign. Seriously, she's a complete creative genius."

"We're all doing our bit," I said quickly, trying to get the attention away from me.

"Yes, but you're coming up with all the best ideas. We're just following your orders. Rob, you know how you were on about getting some fresh ideas for the restaurant? You should really talk to Jess about it."

"Luce, the restaurant is fine as it is," I replied. "Your brother doesn't need any help from me with that."

"Actually, I am looking for some new ideas so if you can suggest anything, I'm willing to listen," he said offhandedly before cutting into his chicken.

To be completely honest, I had a million ideas for the restaurant. Ever since I had been working there I had started storing ideas at the potential that place could unleash. Since Deja Vintage had completely unlocked my business brain again, I had so many ideas whirling around for the restaurant that I was struggling to keep from blurting them out to random people in the street. Despite this new kind of almost-friendship with Rob, I still wasn't convinced he would be happy if I started throwing all these ideas at him for a business he had built up from scratch with his own blood, sweat and tears.

To steer the topic away from what ideas I may or may not have for places of business, I started asking Lucy about her wedding plans. She had mentioned something about starting to look at venues as they wanted to get married next April and since it was less than a year away, places were going to start getting booked up quickly. Thankfully this was another topic she could quite happily talk about and soon all the attention was off me.

After eating enough food to keep me full for at least a week, Lucy and John cleared the dinner plates away so she could bring out the almond cheesecake she had made that afternoon. The two of them carried the dirty plates into the kitchen, refusing any help as apparently Rob and I were guests.

"How do I politely refuse food she's slaved over all afternoon?" I asked Rob.

To my immense surprise, he smiled at me. That was two whole smiles in one evening he had directed at me and I didn't know how to react. Apart from thinking that he had a really nice smile, which I shouldn't be thinking at all.

"You don't. You eat it, enjoy it and maybe don't eat tomorrow."

"How does she keep her shape when she eats that well?"

"Italian metabolism." He shrugged. "Back to the ideas for the restaurant, I was being serious. It's been stuck at a comfortable level for a while and I think it's time to up my game a little, now I can. If you have any ideas, I do want to hear them."

"I have loads," I blurted out.

"Funnily enough, that doesn't surprise me," he said, the smile not leaving his face. This must have been some kind of smiling record for him.

I couldn't help myself, I started smiling back. That kind of idiotic smile you do when faced with an infectious smile from someone else. But while all this was going on, I found myself noticing little things about him like how straight and white his teeth were and how his hair seemed a little longer than normal so it was starting to curl at ends.

This was all stuff I had absolutely no right to start noticing at all.

"It's probably easier if I type some stuff up instead of just throwing ideas at you," I said quickly, trying to get my mind back on the task at hand. "Is there anything specific you want to expand?"

As we made small talk and Rob mentioned a couple of his own ideas, it struck me that Lucy and John were taking a really long time with the plates.

"Would you be open to starting something up on another site?" I asked, only half able to concentrate on what he was talking about. The other half of my attention fell onto his arms. He had started gesturing with his hands quite a lot and I suddenly became very aware of the flex in muscle poking out from under the short sleeves of his t-shirt. Was it common for all chefs to have good biceps and defined forearms because of lifting so many pots and pans?

"Dessert is served," Lucy practically sang as she and John came back to the table. And not a moment too soon. My thoughts were veering into dangerous and confusing territory.

I was having weird flashbacks of my first dinner here when Rob was having a weird effect on me but that was quickly remedied when I'd come to the wrong conclusion that he was gay. What I needed right now was Lucy to reveal something about her brother that would immediately diffuse this situation. Or for Rob to stop being so nice and become that grumpy arse he was when I first met him. I would take either option right now.

"Are you ok Jess?" Lucy asked, clear concern on her face and she slipped a slice of cheesecake in front of me.

"Yeah," I said quickly. "Fine. Why do you ask?"

"Your cheeks have gone all red."

Now my thoughts were seeping through my skin. Perfect. "No, I'm fine. It's probably the fact that we actually hit double figures with the temperature for the first time in forever and I'm unused to not being freezing. I can't cope."

"I'm so glad we're actually seeing some signs of Spring now, even if it is nearly two months late coming," Lucy said as she finished handing out cheesecake and took her own seat.

Yes. Weather was a safe, boring topic. We needed to stick to that and when we had exhausted that conversation piece, I could ask her about her cheesecake recipe which would lead to a food tangent and I would continue to remain safe.

"That cheesecake was amazing Luce," I said, completely ignoring the fact I was full to bursting and forced myself to eat every crumb. "I'll give you a hand with the plates."

"No, no. John will help. You two stay where you are and we'll tidy up. Just carry on talking about whatever it was you were talking about before," she said with an overly bright smile as she nudged John away from the table.

Oh my God. It finally hit me. Lucy was trying to force me and Rob to have some alone time. That was why it had taken her so long in the kitchen before and why she had to take John with her. Now I gave it some thought, I realised she had been trying to set me up with her brother all this time, pushing us together when she had the chance. How had I not seen it before? She had hardly been subtle about the whole thing now I had the luxury of hindsight.

It was a terrible idea. Surely Lucy knew that, considering it was clear as day Rob clearly didn't fancy me. The biggest problem of all though? I wasn't entirely convinced I could say the same for myself.

Chapter 15

My head was a complete muddle and, for the first time since starting at the restaurant, I was dreading going to work. Thankfully, I wasn't down to work a Monday shift, which had given me time to get my thoughts in order. Not so thankfully, I hadn't utilised my time properly and managed to get my thoughts in order.

Clearly it was just the fact I was single, following being in a mismatched relationship for too long, and now Rob was actually acting like a nice person, some strange evolutionary process was making me see him in a different light. I just needed to get him out of my head and maybe meet some more men to show this process that I actually had options again.

Easier said than done because it seemed all roads led back to Rob at the moment. Aside from the fact I worked for him and his sister was one of my best friends, I had spent my entire Monday evening typing up all the ideas I had for his restaurant and organised them in a folder so they were well presented.

I was up at my normal early morning time and feeling fresh – a regular occurrence these days. When I was back in London, I'd have to hit snooze at least four times and would drag my lazy arse out of bed, feeling groggy. Here I was up at the first note of birdsong and greeting the day with the same kind of sickening enthusiasm of a Disney princess. Ok, so maybe I wasn't *that* cheerful and I certainly wasn't singing to any woodland creatures, but I was up and ready to hit the day. More importantly, I was actually looking forward to the day. After a good breakfast, I'd sit down with our Deja Vintage folder and work on that until I had to head to the restaurant.

Though Tuesdays were slightly different.

Riley would be around for his weekly attack on the garden and it had become a routine that he would knock on the kitchen window as he headed into the back garden, giving me a big wave and an even bigger dimpled smile. I would then make us both a cup of tea, dig out a couple of biscuits, and we'd chat in the garden while he pulled up weeds, pruned the rose bushes and anything else Gran entrusted him to do with her precious garden.

Each week we'd talk about the new places he'd decided to add to his ever-growing list for his summer adventure and, more recently, I would talk about the ideas I'd had for the shop, no matter how farfetched some of them were becoming.

"What's going to happen with the waitressing?" he asked as he stuck a spade into a patch of soil and brought his foot down on it.

"I'm going to start phasing it out. The shop will gradually take over more of my time as I cut my hours back with Rob until I'm eventually gone."

"Are you going to miss it?"

I thought for a second at his question then smiled. "Yeah. I think I will."

Even though I'd only been working there for a couple of months, I felt very much at home. I'd bonded quickly with the other staff and had genuinely enjoyed the hours I spent there. Being constantly around customers had also helped my confidence levels get back up to what they were before London. It was going to be hard to walk away from that environment.

"If you're going to be gone soon, I better come in and see what all the fuss is about sooner rather than later. Anything you recommend I order?"

I had absolutely no hesitation in making a suggestion. "The tiramisu. It's an old family recipe apparently, but Rob added something extra which makes it taste like heaven. I have no idea what the secret ingredient is."

A few weeks back, I'd dared to make the comment that, while it was probably very good, it couldn't be good as Lucy's since her tiramisu was one of the most amazing things I'd ever tasted. Rob had simply shrugged it off and just after my shift had ended, he presented me with a box of leftovers and said that he hoped I enjoyed eating my words as much as I enjoyed eating the best tiramisu I would ever taste.

I started my next shift by apologising for doubting his dessert prowess.

"On that note," I said, looking down at my watch, "I better get ready for work. Since we've been blessed with sunshine for a change, I'm going to walk to the restaurant."

"Just the lunch time shift today?"

I nodded as I picked up our empty mugs and said what had now become our Tuesday sign-off, "Same time next week?"

Riley seemed to hesitate for a second before smiling and said, "Have fun at work."

I loaded the mugs into the dishwasher before heading upstairs to change into my waitressing gear. After a quick goodbye to Gran, I stepped back out into the fresh, warm air and set off for the restaurant.

Tina was already there when I arrived and we had a quick chat in the little room where we kept our things when we were on shift before getting ready for the afternoon ahead.

Business slowly trickled in at twelve and remained steady right though until about half three, thanks to a group of workers who were enjoying an extended lunch break to celebrate some big deal they had brokered for their company. My shift was due to end at four and things were calming down nicely as I started to wind down myself.

Table four became occupied, one of only two in the whole restaurant, and I headed over with notepad in hand, ready to take the man's order.

"Good afternoon. Are you ready to order or do you need…Riley?"

The messy mop of blonde hair looked up from the menu on the table and sure enough, Riley was grinning up at me. "I have it on good authority the tiramisu is an excellent choice."

"You came here to order dessert on my recommendation?" I asked with a raised eyebrow as I scribbled his order down on my pad.

"And I wanted to see what all the fuss was about before you left the place."

"Well this is it," I said, gesturing around with my arms. "It's not much, but it's home. Can I get you something to drink?"

He ordered himself a cappuccino, so after I passed his tiramisu request through to the kitchen, I fired up our beast of a coffee machine.

Rob had been a complete dictator when it came to mastering the art of coffee but eventually I had the hang of it and now had mad barista skills. I was even at the stage where I could put little shapes into the cappuccinos as I added the milk and they even looked like what they were supposed to be. And I had to admit, the coffee was so much better with the grounded beans and made, to quote Rob, "*the Italian way*".

The tiramisu was plated not long after I delivered Riley's drink to him, so after taking it out, I left him to it, saying I would check in afterwards to make sure it was as good as expected.

The only other occupied table were now finishing and I cleared their plates as Tina went to sort their bill out and headed back into the kitchen where Rob was using the lull to get things tidied up as they prepared for the next wave at dinner time.

"All done?" he asked, glancing up at the clock as I carried the empty dessert plates over to the dishwasher.

Though it had been a relatively steady afternoon, Rob looked as relaxed as he normally did when in his kitchen. Even when it was packed and we were run off our feet, he was always calm, unflustered and apparently immune to the heat of the kitchen. And his chef whites always stayed pristine. The pasta sauce was probably too scared to rebel.

"I think so, unless you've got anything else you need doing?"

"No. Gethin's just turned up so you're free."

"I've actually got that business expansion info if you want to take it before I head off?"

"That would be great. Do you want to bring it into the office, if you don't have to run off for anything straight away? I'd like to go through it while you're here too. I'll pay you the overtime," he added quickly.

"Erm, sure." Great. Putting myself in an enclosed space with Rob obviously wasn't going to mess with my head at all. "But what about the kitchen?"

"Leo's still here. We've got no open orders now the lunch rush is over, so he'll cope if someone does turn up."

He must have translated the way I was gawping at him was because of complete shock as he then defensively asked, "What?"

"Nothing! It's just that, well, you don't really like to leave Leo unsupervised," I said in a whisper, glancing over at Leo on the other side of the kitchen doing some food prep.

"He's come into his own recently and I wanted to give him some more responsibility." At the sight of my raised eyebrows, he sighed and lowered his voice too, just in case Leo picked anything up. "Fine. *He* wants some more responsibility and drove a pretty hard bargain to get it. But he has come into his own so I'm going to leave him alone for the odd quiet shift and see how he gets on."

"Look at you, delegating," I smiled.

"I only said we'd see. But if any of your ideas are any good, I'll probably have to delegate a lot more, so I had better get used to it."

I was confident enough in my own ideas that he would find at least one he liked. So, with a slightly faster heart rate at the anticipation of having my work reviewed, I grabbed my folder before meeting him in his office where he'd squeezed another chair around his side of the desk.

Fan-effing-tastic.

I really was going to be all by myself in an enclosed space with Rob.

It was so enclosed in fact, that when he stopped flicking through the folder to turn slightly and ask me a question about it, our knees would brush together. It was simple knee-to-knee contact, but with me being a complete mess, it was driving me mad.

"How do you know about this?" he asked, pointing to the top of his current page.

I ignored the knee contact and focused on the paper in front of me. "Oh, I trained through Italy with a couple of friends after the second year of Uni finished and we pretty much did that every night. We thought it was a great concept and a cheap way to eat, since we were on a budget. To save on funds, we'd sometimes sneak some extra food and keep it for breakfast the next day," I added with a fond smile at the memory of how clichéd we were. Penniless students making our way across a foreign country.

"You've been to Italy? Why didn't you ever mention it?"

I shrugged. "I didn't think you required wait staff who had been to Italy. I mean, Graham works here and I don't think he's ever left the country."

"Graham? He's never left the county," he said with a joking glint in his eye I'd never seen before. "Where did you travel to?"

"Started in Venice, then Verona, looped across to Milan then down to Florence and Rome before finishing up in Naples."

Rob actually looked impressed. "And you had an apperitivo or two during this time?"

I laughed as I remembered how much food we'd managed to pack away in those few weeks. "Yep. But we only ever went to the buffet ones so we could get our ten euros worth. That's what I thought would be good restaurant, especially on Monday nights to boost numbers."

"Is that why you mention student nights here?"

"Exactly. Put an apperitivo night on, advertising it as an authentic Italian dining experience and charge a tenner, but do it for eight for the students. They'll all be out in town anyway as Monday's are officially student nights in the bars and clubs, but if they can get a drink and unlimited buffet for under a tenner, they'll come here first to line their stomachs."

"Luce was right; you are an absolutely genius with this stuff." His praise made my chest tighten. "There's some great ideas in here but the apperitivo night is something we can implement straight away. In fact, it's something I can leave Leo with since it'll just be cooking a buffet-sized portions of the general Italian cuisine."

I felt like we were having a real bonding moment just as someone knocked on the door, completely breaking the spell.

"Sorry guys." Graham's head popped around the door. "Jess, there's a guy at table four who said he was waiting for you to finish your shift. He just ordered his third coffee, so I thought I'd let you know before all that caffeine hits the poor bloke."

Table four? That was Riley. But why was he hanging around waiting for me?

"Thanks Graham. Tell him I won't be long."

"Sorry, I've kept you longer than I should have," Rob said as he started putting all the papers to right, though I noticed he was looking more than a little annoyed. Probably because someone was still occupying a table that a new customer could be using, even if it was our afternoon quiet-before-the-storm period.

"No, it's fine; it's only Riley."

"Your gran's gardener?" he said quickly, apparently recognising the name.

"Yeah. Do you know him too?"

"No. Lucy mentioned him once and I guess the name stuck. Anyway, you better go; you don't want to keep him waiting."

It sounded like I was being dismissed and I was so close to giving him a sarcastic curtsey on my way out but he wouldn't have noticed anyway since his focus was back on the folder.

I quickly gathered up my bag from the staff cupboard and headed back into the restaurant, waving to Gethin and Joe on my way past and took the seat opposite Riley on his table.

"I heard you were still hanging around, bringing down the level of our clientele."

"That's me," he shrugged as he drained his cup of coffee. "I actually have a proposal for you."

"Nothing gardening based I hope. I'm about as good at gardening as I am at sewing."

"Nah, something better than that." He stood up and pulled a twenty pound note out of his back pocket, waving at Joe before signalling he was leaving it on the table. "Cheers mate."

"I didn't realise gardening was such a lucrative business to leave tips like that," I joked as we stepped outside onto the street.

"It isn't normally but your Gran was pretty generous with my leaving tip, bless her heart, so I thought I should pay a little of that forward for good karma."

I stopped dead. "Leaving tip?"

Riley turned back to face me, looking a little uncomfortable. "Erm, yeah, today was my last time doing her garden. New bloke starts next week. She said she wanted to contribute to my travel fund to make sure I had the time of my life."

That sounded exactly like Gran.

"I didn't realise you were leaving already. When do you go?"

"Friday."

"Friday!" I thought I had more time to prepare to say goodbye. There was certainly going to be a void in my Tuesday mornings now. "Why didn't you say before?"

"I didn't really know how to come out with it to be honest. Plus, well, I wanted to see if you wanted to come with me."

"Travelling?"

"Yeah. Think about it, in a week you could be in Greece island hopping or we could be eating pizza in Naples. The world is our oyster; we'll go where the wind takes us. Every time I mentioned a new place I wanted to go, you kept saying how jealous you were."

"But I'm supposed to be sorting out a business," I pointed out, still recovering from the shock of what he was asking.

"It won't be forever, just for the summer. You can still plan as we travel. All you need to do is pack a bag and we're ready to go. Think about all the fun we could have."

I'd be lying if I said the thought hadn't crossed my mind a few times after he'd listed off where he was going to go and what he was going to do. I always tried to picture myself doing what he was going to do; just heading off into the great unknown and doing whatever I felt like whenever I wanted.

We probably could have a lot of fun. Fun any other girl in my shoes would jump at the chance of having with this attractive Aussie on a beach in Spain or a cobbled street in France.

But the pictures of all this adventure were never of me. I could never place myself doing all of that.

"I'm sorry Riley but I can't do it."

That was the truth; I really couldn't do it. Backpacking, wandering, adventuring? That wasn't me. If he had a set plan of where he was going to go, where he was going to stay and how long for, then maybe I would have been tempted to say yes. Now I had control over my life again, I had realised that I liked it. I liked knowing what was what, and yes, boring as it sounded, I liked routine. At this time in my life, I was craving stability and order. Gallivanting across Europe with a handsome nomad was not going to get me that.

"You wouldn't want to travel with me anyway," I added. "I'd complain a lot and slow you down. You'd probably want to strangle me before we were even off the plane. I'm sorry, but that kind of thing just isn't me. You'll find some fun people along the way who are more like you and you'll be thankful I didn't tag along."

"I really doubt that. But no worries. I thought I'd ask anyway though I kind of knew what your answer would be," he said with a sad smile. "I guess this is goodbye...for now."

He opened his arms and pulled me into a tight bear hug.

"Good luck Riley," I said as I hugged him back. "Take care and send postcards. Just because I'm not the adventurous type doesn't mean I can't live vicariously through you."

"If you change your mind..." he trailed off as he pulled back.

I shook my head. "I can't guarantee anything. I feel like my future is here and I have everything I need right now."

"That's because you're one of these proper adults who has their shit together."

And as we said our final goodbyes and parted ways, I couldn't help feeling that that was the best compliment I may have ever received.

Chapter 16

"Tina, what's wrong?"

I'd just finished my lunch time shift and was getting ready to leave the evening shift to the second wave of staff, excited at the prospect of having the house to myself. Olive had persuaded Gran to head to Brighton for the weekend, so I was going to have a long bath followed by a Scandal binge-session. I was very aware that my Gran was much more of a socialite than I was.

But as I was gathering my things together from our little staff room, Tina came in, looking as if she'd seen Death, her phone gripped in her hand.

"Dave just rang to say that Ella fell off the top of the slide at the park and she might have broken something. He's taking her to the hospital now."

"Tina, you have to go up there," Rob said firmly, his head appearing through the door.

"But...but I can't just go." There was a waver in her voice and I could tell she was on the verge of tears. "There's a big party of fifteen coming in at half seven and I can't-."

"I'll cover your shift for you," I cut across her. "And before you even think of arguing with me, I won't be taking no for an answer."

She did look as if she was going to argue but then flung her arms around my neck. "Thanks Jess, you're the best. I promise I'll cover as many of your shifts as you want from now on."

She picked her bag up and ran out of the restaurant, promising to text me when she knew what the situation was with Ella.

"You're sure you don't mind staying? You have been here since eleven already. I don't think I can legally let you work for that long."

"Rob, honestly, it's fine. And I promise I won't report you. Gran's away for the weekend so I'd just be going back to an empty house anyway."

"And there was me thinking you would have some big Saturday night plans."

I couldn't hold in the laugh. "Chance would be a fine thing but apart from work and planning the vintage shop, it seems as if I have no life at the moment."

"The silver lining is that you get to spend your evening with me." The corners of his mouth twitched. "But if you get tired, take a break whenever. And if you get hungry, just shout and I'll whip you something up."

"Just have a lot of coffee on standby."

"You know how to work the machine so I give you permission to help yourself to as much as you can physically handle. But thanks Jess, I really appreciate it." He gave me a smile that lit up his warm eyes, sending a jolt through my stomach. I could only nod in reply as I mentally prepared myself for round two.

"My feet are absolutely killing me."

It was quarter to eleven and I was propping up the bar with my fourth coffee of the evening as Graham cleaned around me and Gethin carried the linens out back to count. They knew I'd done a double shift and both argued that as soon as we'd cleared the last plate away, I wasn't to do anything else. I'd just managed to gently nudge the last of our customers out the door so we could lock up a little early.

"But you look like you did alright on the tip front. And did I see you pick up a few phone numbers too?"

"It was just two," I said with a slightly pleased smile. I wasn't going to call either of them but it had been a great ego boost. And I had forty quid's worth of tips to show for my efforts this evening.

Rob then emerged from the kitchen looking very relaxed for a man who had been cooking non-stop all evening. "Kitchen staff has been released so you are also free to go. Leave whatever you're doing because I'll come in tomorrow and I can finish it up then."

Graham was out of there like a shot saying he could still make a friend's house party, persuading Gethin to join him with the assurance there would be plenty of single women in attendance, but I didn't move because I was too happy to finally be sitting down.

Rob didn't seem in too much of a hurry either, as he cashed up and was actually nice enough to let me finish my drink before setting the alarm and turning all the lights off. We walked out the back together and he held the door open for me, only to reveal it was chucking it down. It was proper April shower weather and we'd had plenty of those during April but since we were almost halfway through May, I was hoping they would have eased off. Apparently not. God bless British weather.

"Are you walking home?"

"It's fine. It's only a bit of rain and I have a coat so don't worry about it Jess."

He made to step outside but I put my arm across the door to stop him. "You are not walking home in this. That's a jacket, not a coat. If you die of pneumonia, Lucy will kill me for having let you walk in this. I'm going to drop you home."

"You're so dramatic. I'll-."

"Don't argue with me. I'm driving you home and that's that."

He grudgingly accepted and I stayed with him until he had locked the back door then we both legged it to the car. I was soaked to the skin after just the short trip.

"Ok, so maybe it's a little heavier than I thought." Rob admitted once we were safely inside the car.

I whacked the heating on full blast and drove through town towards the park with Rob directing me. I pulled up on a street full of Georgian townhouses that looked as if they had been broken up into flats.

"Thanks Jess. I will admit, it was better than walking. And thanks again for the extra shift, I really do appreciate it."

I smiled, proud that I had managed to get a double thank-you out of Roberto Amato but the moment was quickly ruined when my stomach gave a massive and embarrassing growl to complain that I hadn't eaten in almost eleven hours. I felt my cheeks redden immediately.

"Jess, how hungry *are* you?" My embarrassed silence seemed to intensify the annoyed look on his face. "Jesus Jess, I told you as soon as you got hungry to let me know and I'd make you something. It's bad enough that you probably worked an illegal number of hours, but working them on an empty stomach too? Have you actually eaten anything today?"

"I had a sandwich just before I started. What? You were really busy cooking food for actual paying customers so I didn't want to bother you."

He gave a loud sigh as he pinched the bridge of his nose. "Jess, the world is not going to end just because you decide to think about yourself before other people once in a while."

I opened my mouth to argue but the sight of him leaning forward to take off his jacket and passing it across stopped me.

"Put it over your head to keep the rain off. My flat is that one just there. I'll can make you something so you don't pass out on the drive home."

He was already out of the car before I even had a chance to say no.

Having been left with no choice, I held his coat over my head as a makeshift umbrella and got out of the car, running across the road to catch up to him. I reached him as he was fumbling with his keys and tried to cover him with his jacket as well to help keep the rain off, but it seemed pretty pointless now he was drenched. The large front door swung open and we stepped into the dry.

"I've got the ground floor flat, so it's just round here."

He unlocked the door to his left and I followed him in. He took his jacket back and hung it on the hook by the door then led me down the little hallway. I could see that his white t-shirt had now been rendered see-through because of the rain and it clung to his body. I swallowed, trying not to think about it, but it was incredibly hard to ignore the nicely defined muscles on his back.

"What do you want to drink?" he asked, snapping me out of my inappropriate thoughts.

"Water's fine."

"You mean you haven't had enough already?" He filled a glass from the tap and handed it to me. "I'm just going to change into a dry t-shirt then I'll start cooking. Make yourself at home."

I glanced around at his kitchen, surprised by how untidy it was. The kitchen at the restaurant was meticulously organised whereas here, things were lying about waiting to be put away and pieces of paper were scattered everywhere. Some of them were just odd words whereas others were full recipes.

I felt a hand on my shoulder and jumped. I hadn't heard him behind me.

"Sorry. I thought you might want this."

He held up a towel for me. My hair was a little damp so I took the towel and started to blot at the ends of it.

"Right. Let's get some food into you."

"What house speciality do I get?"

"Cheese on toast. The last thing I want to do after a long day of cooking is to make something that requires a lot of effort so we're eating simple."

"Can I do anything to help?"

"Get the cheese out of the fridge and start slicing it."

"Yes chef." I saluted him like we were in the army which actually made him laugh.

As we made the highly sophisticated cheese on toast, well fell into a comfortable silence. There was just something reassuring about his presence and I didn't feel the need to fill the silence with inane chatter.

"How's your sewing going?" he asked as he slid the tray under the grill. "Every time I see Lucy these days she's got a needle in her hands. She really loves it. "

"She should, she's a complete natural. I'm still rubbish at it but I like the sewing bees for the atmosphere. I wouldn't have become friends with Lucy and Ashley without it and it makes Gran really happy. Plus, if there was no sewing bee there would be no vintage shop on the horizon."

"Keeping people happy is important to you, isn't it?"

I leaned against the worktop, crossing my arms to show my annoyance at his tone. "Does this have anything to do with your comment in the car? About how I put other people first - because that's not a bad thing."

"I never said it was." He held his hands up defensively. "But I do think you need to be a little selfish sometimes and think about what you want."

I frowned at him. I was getting annoyed but only because there was a hint of truth in what he was saying. If I was a bit more selfish, maybe I wouldn't have quit my great job without thinking and moved to London with Liam to support him. Then I wouldn't have been so focused on his happiness that I didn't even realise how unhappy I was.

"But it's a good trait to have," Rob said with a soft smile that went right to his eyes. "Shows how much you care about the people you love. You said your gran was away this weekend?"

"She's on a girly weekend in Brighton with one of her friends."

"So your grandmother has more of a social life than you?" he observed as he pulled the tray out from the grill and slid a piece of toast onto a plate for me.

"Thanks." I took a careful bite as it was piping hot. "And yes, Gran does have more of a life than me. Though she's promised to have a hunt around the vintage shops there and see if she can pick up any bargains we can sell on."

"I was surprised you weren't out on a date tonight with one of the many men who have been leaving their phone numbers for you at the restaurant since you started. Or that Aussie guy." There was more of an edge to his tone than usual.

I laughed through another mouthful of cheese and quickly chewed the food I'd practically inhaled so I could answer without spraying him with crumbs. "Riley's not exactly my type, and even if he were, he's off on his grand European tour now anyway. And there were only a couple of men who left their number who probably only did it for a laugh."

"Why is it so difficult for you to accept that a man might actually want to go out with you?"

I set my empty plate down on the worktop. "Oh yeah, a twenty-six-year-old who lives with her grandmother because she can't afford her own place and her last boyfriend found her so boring he had to get his enjoyment elsewhere. I'm a real catch. Who in their right mind would actually want me?"

"I would."

He looked as stunned at the words that had come out of his mouth as I felt hearing them. It didn't make any sense. I thought he didn't even like me.

"I'm sorry Jess, it just slipped out," he said awkwardly, looking anywhere but at me. "I honestly didn't bring you here to confess anything. I did genuinely just want to make you some food. I don't want things to get weird, but you need to realise that you're funny, caring and incredibly beautiful. Any man would be lucky to have you, so please stop putting yourself down."

Somewhere in my mind, as he was talking, his previous comment about thinking about myself and what I wanted appeared. I wanted him and I had for a while, no matter how much I'd tried to convince myself otherwise. So with courage I didn't even know I had, I grabbed the front of his t-shirt and pulled him forward to kiss him. When I felt him kiss me back, pure happiness flooded through my body. Everything else just seemed to melt away and there was only us.

His kiss quickened, sending shivers of delight through my spine as he manoeuvred me between him and the worktop.

"Jess," he whispered, pulling back ever so slightly. "God knows how much I want you to stay, but if this is happening too quickly, tell me to stop and I will."

"Shut up," I answered breathlessly. "This is not the time to be a gentleman."

This was all the invitation he needed. He kissed me again, so deeply it sent shockwaves coursing through my body. All of my senses seemed to have been amplified. He tasted like the coffee he had been drinking all day, he smelt like the rain and he felt so warm and strong underneath my hands. Everything about this seemed so right.

His hands moved across my body and he deftly undid the buttons of my shirt, sliding it off. He guided me out of the kitchen without breaking the kiss and we moved down the hallway, into the bedroom, shedding our clothes and leaving a trail as we went.

What happened next was an absolute revelation.

I always thought those clichés people spouted about great sex was always slightly over exaggerated but that night I felt the Earth move, saw God and all those other things that were supposed to happen, happened. At one point I was calling out every deity's name under the sun.

As our limbs became entangled, it was hard to tell where I started and he began but everything we did was perfectly in sync and completely natural. It was no wonder why women put Italian men at the top of their lists.

We both fell back onto the pillows breathing heavily before I curled up next to him and rested my head on his chest. Once upon a time, I never would have been able to picture myself being here. Now? I didn't want to be anywhere else.

Chapter 17

When I woke the following morning, I could hear the steady patter of rain against the window. Part of me wondered if everything that had happened the night before had been just some wonderful dream my subconscious had concocted to mess with me but when my brain worked out that the weight across my hip was someone's arm, I automatically smiled.

"What are you so happy about?"

I swivelled my body and saw Rob propped up on one elbow, smiling as well. Maybe it was because it took me so long to see that smile, but I thought it only made him more attractive. He needed to smile all the time.

"Oh God, you're not one of those weirdos who watches women sleep, are you?" I teased.

"Only when you're involved." He leant in and brushed his lips lightly against mine which was more than enough to bring images of last night's events to the forefront of my mind. Both the original event and then the repeat performance. "Did you sleep ok?"

"Perfectly. But then, I was pretty tired."

This only amplified the incredible smile on his face and he moved his hand to tuck my hair behind my ear. "Does that mean you're fully rested now?"

The tone of his voice and the intensity of his stare was enough to know what he was suggesting. Who would have guessed that the serious Roberto Amato was really a complete sex-god?

I slipped my arms around his neck to pull him towards me and we made slow, leisurely love – the kind that Sunday mornings were just made for. Afterwards, he almost demanded that I didn't move from the bed while he went to make breakfast, returning with omelette oozing with cheese. I couldn't remember the last time a man had brought me breakfast in bed. It had definitely been a very long time, if it had ever happened at all.

As we were eating, I heard the shrill ringing of a phone that I knew wasn't mine. Rob looked at me when he heard it too, a pure apologetic look in his face. "Sorry. I'll be quick."

He climbed out of bed and picked his jeans up off the floor, fishing around for his phone which he eventually pulled out and answered, "Morning Luce, what's up?"

He climbed back into bed as I froze ever so slightly. Was he going to tell Lucy I was here? I knew she'd be over the moon about the whole thing since she'd been trying to set me up with her brother since day one. But then why would he tell her? Maybe this wasn't actually a thing and it wasn't going to go beyond today. I didn't even know where I stood. I held my breath as I listened to what he was saying while trying to appear nonchalant about the whole thing.

"No Luce, sorry, I have to be at the restaurant for most of today so I can't do dinner." There was a pause from him and I heard Lucy's voice on the other end of the phone although I couldn't make out what she was saying. "Well, she did work an extra shift at the last-minute yesterday so I imagine she's pretty tired and that's probably why she hasn't answered. She might still be asleep."

My heart leapt. They were talking about me.

"No Lucy, I promise I'm not forcing her to work too hard. I'm not the slave driver you think I am." He glanced over at me, his mouth twitching as he slipped his hand under to duvet to give my thigh a squeeze. "I'm almost positive that she's just worn out from last night and needs a bit of time to recover."

I stared at him with my mouth open, wanting so desperately to laugh.

"Yep, ok. Will do. Bye Lucy."

He hung up and put the phone on the bedside cabinet. "Lucy's been trying to call you to invite you round for dinner tonight. I think she was trying to attempt another set-up with me, since she's not one to accept defeat easily. Did you pick up on her subtle hints that was what she was doing?"

"Subtle and Lucy aren't two words I would stick together in the same sentence." Though I neglected to inform him I was a little slow on the uptake.

"I tried to stay away from you, I really did, but it was impossible. I've wanted you since you first caused all those problems in my restaurant that lunchtime."

That day seemed like years ago considering how much everything had changed since. Considering how much I had changed. "You knew I was there?"

"You did kind of stand out in that red dress of yours," he admitted with an embarrassed kind of smile that was utterly adorable.

My heart leapt at the fact he remembered and I made a mental note to wear that dress around him again. "Really? Is that why Lucy forced us together at that dinner?"

"No. She was just desperately trying to set me up with a nice girl and after she met you, she decided you fit the bill."

"Even when it was obvious you hated me?"

He visibly winced at words and I immediately regretted them. "I never hated you Jess. I'm sorry I acted like such a dick around you. You did something to me and it scared me, so I thought if I acted badly around you, you'd want nothing to do with me and it would make things a whole lot easier."

"That was the worst thing you could have done. I have this uncontrollable need to make people like me so the more you acted like you disliked me, the more I wanted to make you like me."

"Well it certainly worked. And because Lucy doesn't understand the meaning of the word no. You have no idea how much torture it was for me when you started at the restaurant. But, honestly, you were a god send so I had to swallow my own selfish needs for the good of my business."

"Sounds like she was lecturing you for making me work too hard."

"If only she knew how true that was." He laughed, his face brightening as the hand that was still on my thigh squeezed again. "You might want to call her back at some point. But if she invites you round for dinner, tell her you're busy."

That surprised me slightly. "Why? Will I be busy?"

"You will. You're going to meet me at the restaurant at four. I definitely think I need to cook you a proper dinner. Cheese on toast was not good enough."

Delight swept through my body. It didn't sound like it was going to be a one-night-thing. But I tried to not show the elation that filled me too much, so I responded coyly, "Well, maybe. But Lucy was going to offer to cook and I think she's the better chef in the family."

He leaned in to kiss me. "Not funny. So, you'll be there at four?"

It was my turn to kiss him. "I suppose I can make it."

"I'll make it worth your while, I promise. And without sounding like a massive arse, I think I need to kick you out soon. I didn't realise how late it was and I need to go sort out some things at the restaurant before you turn up or you'll end up having to help me with boring paperwork."

I could hardly take offense to that. Plus, it would give me a chance to go home and freshen up. I also made a mental note to call Lucy when I got home as well because I had the feeling if I called her while Rob was around, he might try to put me off for his own amusement.

Throwing on my work clothes from the night before, I left his flat and headed home, calling Lucy as soon as I walked through the door. It felt awful having to lie to her but I stuck with the story Rob had come up with, saying that I had slept in late because I'd done back to back shifts and was shattered. It felt even worse lying to her that I couldn't make it to dinner because I was spending time with Gran this evening when she got home. Dragging Gran into the lie probably wasn't the best move, but I knew they would both forgive me when they knew the situation.

I spent the afternoon catching up on a bit of housework I hadn't been able to do yesterday then took that long bath, putting in the extra effort to exfoliate and moisturise in preparation for later. By quarter to four, I had changed three times and agonised about whether to have my hair up or down. I wasn't even sure why I was feeling nervous about this. We had already slept together, three times in the space of however many hours without any influence of alcohol, so there wasn't really anything I could do to surprise him, but even thinking of it this way did nothing to stop the butterflies fluttering about in my stomach.

In the end, I had decided on one of Gran's floral fifties dresses because it had now stopped raining and I could wear ballet pumps and cardigan with it. The nipped-in waist made my already small one look tiny but the flared skirt at least made it look like I had hips and gave me some kind of shape. I pulled my hair back into a low ponytail, just to make it look like I hadn't tried too hard even though I so had.

I left a note for Gran to say I was going to be out for the evening and not to worry if I was late back then I drove down to the restaurant. Parking up in my normal spot, I knocked on the back door as I walked through and called out to Rob. I heard an echoed response saying he was in the kitchen. It was eerily quiet and felt strange being here knowing no one else was and that I wasn't getting ready to work.

I popped my head around door and saw Rob standing at one of the stations, a light dusting of flour already on his black t-shirt. He smiled as he saw me and my heart fluttered.

"What are you making?" I asked as I walked towards him, putting my bag on the side.

"Correction, what are *we* making." He wiped his hands on a tea towel so he could cup my face to kiss me.

"I have to make dinner myself? You brought me here under false pretences. I'm leaving," I said in a faux-outraged voice.

I was about to dramatically storm off but he caught me around the waist. "It'll be completely worth it. Now put on an apron."

He handed me a white apron which I put on then rolled the sleeves of my cardigan up. "So what are you expecting me to make?"

"Homemade pizza. I've got everything ready; just wash your hands first."

Always the professional.

I went over to the sink and washed my hands so not the lower the perfect hygiene rating of his restaurant then stood next to him. He slid a bowl covered in a damp tea towel over to me. "Here's one I prepared earlier. I had to let it rise for an hour but you get the fun job of kneading it."

He sprinkled some flour onto the counter and put the dough on top of it, then stepped aside to let me take over. I tentatively started to roll the dough around in the flour then pushed my hands into it. I heard Rob chuckle besides me.

"What?"

"You don't have to be so delicate. Really go for it. Pretend it's Liam's face."

The fact he mentioned Liam caught me off guard for a second but it turned out to be good advice. Visualising that I was hitting Liam in the face was an effective way of kneading dough. As I worked through the dough, apparently to the point where it should look shiny and smooth, Rob struck up conversation.

"Did you speak to Lucy?" he asked as he casually leaned against the worktop with his arms folded.

I dug the heels of my hands into the dough. "I did. I told her that I'd slept late because I was shattered. I said you were a horrible boss taking advantage of my kind nature and keeping me longer than necessary."

I glanced up at him and he was looking decidedly smug. "Believe me, it was completely necessary. Did she try to invite you to dinner?"

"Yep. I told her I was spending the evening with Gran so I couldn't go. I think she believed me."

His smile vanished and he looked serious, although it was a softer type of seriousness than I usually saw on him. "I'm sorry you had to lie. But to be honest, I'm not too sure how to handle this. Lucy will make a massive thing out of it when we tell her."

"What are we telling her?" I tried to keep my voice steady and casual.

His lips twitched. "I don't know. I suppose be honest and tell her the truth about whatever this is. What do you want this to be?"

He was throwing the ball into my court and giving me the power here. I didn't know if that was a good thing or a bad thing, but the one thing I was sure of was that I needed to answer it honestly. "I want this to be something."

"Good answer," he said as his face broke into a smile. "But I'll let you be the one to tell her. You can handle her crazy reaction better than I probably will."

"Well, we'll see about that. Is the dough done yet because my hands are starting to ache?"

"You're about half way there."

"What? Now I know how you ended up with impressive arms."

He edged in towards me. "You think my arms are impressive do you?"

I pushed him away with one hand, leaving some dough remnants on his t-shirt. "Oh shut up. Finish the dough for me because I'm getting hungry."

I scooted to the side and let him get on with it, watching him for the pro he was. Once he was satisfied with it, he took a rolling pin and rolled it out into the shape he wanted, although it didn't look like a very big pizza.

"Right, your turn again and this is the fun bit. You get to toss the base."

"Really? I've always wanted to do that. But I will end up with it on the floor, so I hope you've got a spare."

"Not with me here you won't," he said confidently and he handed me the dough and put his hands on my hips to pull me away from the counter. "Just remember not to throw it very high if you think you're going to drop it. Always keep your fingers closed otherwise you'll just put a hole in the dough and you want to try and throw it so it's on its side, not flat, catching it with the heel of your hand. You ready?"

I took a deep breath but the fact he was stood so close behind me, one hand still on my hip and the other one around me to try and set my arm right, was very distracting. I gave it a go anyway. Lowering my arm slightly, I then brought it back up quickly making the dough spin a couple of inches in the air. I caught it again without splitting the dough and let out a laugh. "I did it! And I didn't drop it."

"That's good. Now this time, try and go a little higher."

With a rush of confidence, I threw it again, higher than before and managed to catch it right. I carried on doing this, getting braver each time with the height until Rob told me I could stop and it finally looked like a large pizza base. Setting it back down on the counter, he walked over to the fridge and returned with a couple of containers.

"First, you need to put the sauce on. Pour it in the middle and then kind of swirl it around towards the edges."

I took the ladle, filling it with the sauce and Rob stood behind me, his head above my shoulder so we were almost cheek to cheek and closed his hand over the top of mine to manoeuvre it. Once the sauce had been spread, he stood back and pointed at the other containers, each covered in cling film.

"Four cheeses. I'm guessing that the Quattro Formaggi is your favourite as it's the only pizza I've seen you eat."

I nodded, unable to say anything because a small lump had formed in my throat. It was only something tiny, but the fact he had noticed it meant a lot to me.

"Ricotta goes on first, then just chuck some of the mozzarella and gorgonzola on. Top it all off with parmesan."

"Chuck? Is that the professional term in the restaurant industry?"

"It is in my kitchen."

I added the cheese to the pizza, going heavy with the mozzarella and then let Rob slide it onto the tray, putting it into the wood oven. I knew how much effort went into prepping the wood oven, so the fact he had gone to all that trouble just for one pizza was very touching.

"In eight minutes, you will be eating the first pizza you ever made yourself. Not a bad first attempt." He gave me a light kiss then took my hand. "Come with me, the next bit is the most important."

He led me through to the restaurant where he'd already set a table up for us. The plates and cutlery had been laid out, along with a bottle of red wine. The blinds had been drawn so it was a little too dark but he pulled a lighter out of his pocket and lit the taper in the Chianti bottle, engulfing the table in a warm glow.

He picked the bottle off the table and held it up for me. "I thought a bottle of Barbera d'Alba would do us nicely, if that's ok?"

"Sounds perfect. What do you want me to do?"

"Absolutely nothing. Just sit down and enjoy being waited on for a change."

He poured the wine then disappeared back into the kitchen, returning a couple of minutes later with our pizza, setting it down in the middle of the table. I noticed he'd sprinkled rocket on the top to give it a little colour.

He sat himself down in his seat and picked up his wine glass. "*Buon appetito!*"

I repeated the phrase in my terrible non-Italian accent and clinked my glass against his before diving into the pizza. I took a bite, feeling famished, having not eaten since breakfast. "This is so good. My compliments to the chef."

He shrugged. "It's alright I suppose."

181

I playfully kicked him under the table but he just smiled and ran his foot up my leg in retaliation.

Without wanting to ruin the moment we were having, there had been something that had been playing on my mind since I arrived so I thought it would be best to mention it sooner rather than later. "Rob, if we tell Lucy that we're now seeing each other, it's going to become public knowledge pretty quickly. Are you allowed to be involved with one of your staff? I mean, do you have any rules about it?"

His brow furrowed as he helped himself to a slice of pizza. "Well, no, but then I've never been attracted to one of my staff before."

"What about Sally?" I blurted out without thinking.

Rob seemed surprised I had mentioned her name but at least he didn't look angry. "Fair point. It was never an issue, until the, well, you know…At the end of the day, I'm the boss so I think that gives me license to do what I want."

"Do you think they will be ok with it? They won't resent me because, well…"

"Because you're sleeping with the boss?" he finished for me.

I smiled at the bluntness of it. "Well, yeah."

He reached across the table, taking hold of one of my hands. "I hardly think anyone will be too bothered by it since they all love you anyway but you're not going to be here all that long as it is."

My body stiffened. Was he going to sack me so we could carry on sleeping together? Maybe that was the only way we could properly make a go of this, although I wasn't sure I was entirely comfortable with that.

"Jess, I'm not going to sack you."

"How did you know that's what I was thinking?"

"You have a very readable face," he replied with a little smile. "What I meant is this job is only temporary for you, we both knew that when I hired you. It was a temporary arrangement and we were both doing each other a favour. You're going to start putting in more of your time in getting the shop up and running, eventually making it full time because it's in your own interest to do so."

I let out a sigh of relief. "Sorry. I hadn't even considered that."

"You worry too much. Now eat some more pizza before it gets cold."

I picked up another slice, the melted cheese stringing out as I raised it to my mouth. Without blowing my own horn, it was pretty amazing. We ate with a comfortable air around us, talking about the plans Rob had for the restaurant and my plans for the shop.

When we'd finished, I insisted on playing the waitress and clearing the plates away – it was the very least I could do. I quickly washed the plates up as Rob tidied our table in the restaurant and it was if we had never been there.

I drove us to his flat and we spent the rest of the evening there.

Chapter 18

"Jess, can I see you in the office please. Now."

"Ooh, what have you done now you little trouble maker?" Graham grinned up at me from his position on the floor, restocking the wine bottles.

We'd had a quiet Monday evening at the restaurant and the last of the diners were out the door by nine, so we were using the lull to get everything behind the bar properly restocked and in order.

"Dunno, could be anything knowing me," I grinned back. "Sure you can cope without adult supervision for a while?"

"It'll be hard but I'll try to behave."

I stepped out from behind the bar and headed towards Rob's office, almost certain that it wasn't because I was in trouble.

For two weeks we had managed to keep our budding relationship secret from everyone. As much as I hated lying to Gran and my friends, I had to admit, there was something thrilling about all the sneaking around, which had included quite a few stolen moments in the office.

As soon as I closed the door behind me, Rob had me pressed up against it and was kissing me in a way that made me go completely light-headed – a regular occurrence these days.

"I know I shouldn't, but I've started to appreciate the early eaters on a Monday night. It gives me more time for things like this."

"It's bad for business," I replied as I wrapped my arms around his neck.

"But it's good for me. I've given Leo the lunchtime shift tomorrow if you're free to come over?"

Since we'd been trying not to draw any attention to ourselves, I hadn't been able to spend the night at Rob's because Gran would start asking questions if she worked out that I wasn't sleeping in my own bed. So we had to try and plan our time together. Sometimes I would go back to his and we'd have a few hours together before I headed home, passing the lateness off as being stuck sorting things at work. Other times, we would sneak away together in the afternoons now Rob had enough faith in Leo to handle the kitchen by himself.

"If anyone asks, I'm heading into town to sort a few things out before my shift starts."

"Are you getting as fed up with all the sneaking around as I am?" he asked softly as he tucked the piece of hair that had fallen loose from my clip, behind my ear.

"I don't like the lying," I admitted. "I'm so bad at it, I'm sure I'm going to slip up soon."

"That's because you're not a born liar. You're a good person." His compliment warmed me right through to my fingertips. Considering what he'd been through after being repeatedly lied to by a woman, I was happy he didn't think me capable of deceiving people. "And I don't want to keep you trapped in my flat. I want to be able to go out to the cinema instead of using Netflix. God help me but I even want to have couple evenings with Lucy and John."

"She's going to plan so many when she finds out," I teased.

He rolled his beautiful brown eyes. "I know she will, but it's something I'm willing to endure."

I smiled as I dug my hands into his hair to pull his head down for another kiss, using my last ounce of self-control to stop when things got a bit too heated. "So I tell Lucy when I next see her?"

"Yep. We're going public. Now you better get out of here before I change my mind and demand you work overtime."

I threw a wink over my shoulder as I left his office then worked the remainder of my shift and forced myself out of the restaurant, knowing I would see Lucy the following evening at the sewing bee and I still had enough time to prepare what I was going to say to her.

At least I thought I had.

My plans were completely thrown out the next morning when I headed downstairs, all ready with my *going to town to run errands* excuse, to find both Lucy and Ashley at the kitchen table, enjoying a cup of tea with Gran.

"There you are," Ashley said almost impatiently. "We thought you'd never come downstairs. Are you ready?"

"Ready for what?" I asked, completely oblivious to whatever was going on.

"Didn't you get my text? I think I've found a potential shop space and we've got an appointment at eleven to have a look."

Now I was a little less bewildered, I properly looked at my friends. Ashley was dressed like she meant business, even with the baby bump. I knew her well enough now to know when she was about to project her confidence to intimidate people which was probably going to help us with the Letting Agent. If this failed, Lucy just looked her usual beautiful self which would be enough to distract the Letting Agent, if we had a male one, into hopefully giving us a good deal.

"Really? I haven't checked my phone this morning." I was too pre-occupied preparing for another secret meeting at Rob's. Oh, right. "Erm, I was supposed to run some errands this morning in town. Can you give me a sec to rearrange?"

"Rob's not going to care if you cancel on him when it's about a shop space. You two can meet any time."

I felt my jaw hit the kitchen floor as I looked at Lucy, who was pretending to inspect her nails before smiling at me.

"How, I mean...when?"

"I figured it out a week ago," Lucy said casually. "But your gran worked it out before I did."

"You really thought you could keep secrets from me Jessica?" Gran said in her stern voice, but I could see her fighting a smile which relaxed me a little.

"I guess the cat's out of the bag now," I shrugged, wondering where I'd slipped up when I thought I was being so careful. "Let me call him now then."

I fished my phone out of my bag and saw Ashley's message but ignored it and rang Rob, who picked up on the second ring. "Hey, it's me. I can't make it this morning; Ash has found us a potential space for the shop so we're going to look at that. And by the way, everyone already knew about us apparently."

He was silent for a second then asked me to pass the phone over to his sister, which I did, listening to her end of the conversation. "Oh Rob, you're so naïve.... don't worry, I'm sure you'll get over it...No, I won't interrogate her too much...ok...ok...*ok*...ciao."

She hung up and handed the phone back to me, grinning from ear to ear. "We'll talk about all this later as I will require you to fill in the blanks for me at some point. But first, we have a shop to check out."

I breathed out a sigh of relief, feeling lighter that I didn't have to lie to my friends anymore, and that I didn't have to plan my speech on what had been going on. At least the hard part was done now.

Jumping into Lucy's car and heading into town, Ashley began to fill me in on what she'd found. Since we were going to promote the tea room as much the vintage shop as our figures had this down as a good little earner for us, Ashley had been keeping her eye out for the perfect space to accommodate both of these. As much as we all wanted to get the shop up and running, we'd all agreed that we wait until we had found the perfect premises, even if it took longer than planned.

"The property used to be an old café," Ashley said as she spread herself out on the back seat. "From the info I saw online, it had two rooms to it. If my planning is right, which obviously it will be, the main café side with the kitchen area and counters will do us for the tea room while the other room, which is the bigger of the two, will be perfect for the shop."

"Sounds good to me," I replied. "And this is probably better than finding a shop-shop then adding the tea room stuff into it."

"Exactly. It's easier to take stuff out we don't need than adding everything new into it. Though I have no idea what kind of state this kitchen will be in since apparently this property has been on the market for eighteen months, which means I should be able to negotiate the rent."

Lucy took her eyes off the road for a second to grin at me. We'd both said before we wished we'd had a chance to see City Ashley. Our Ashley was still tough when she needed to be but was a big softie inside. City Ashley on the other hand was probably a complete ball-breaker. Hopefully we could have a nice combination of the two today.

We ended up down one of the cobbled side-roads off from the main high street, just outside the shop space. Being able to park, for free, down that street was going to be a plus for customer flow.

"Good location," Ashley said as she assessed the front of the shop's slightly warn façade. You could tell it had been unoccupied for a while. "There's no other cafes on the street from what I can see but they all seems to be independent shops, which fits with our thinking. Nothing vintage style either so that's good."

As we climbed out of the car, a middle-aged man immediately came through the door of the shop to greet us. He had a friendly enough look to him and didn't appear to be the type of Letting Agent to press us too much. Though I was more than confident Ashley was going to shoot down anything she didn't think was going to benefit us.

"Good morning ladies. My name is Don Campbell. Which one of you is Mrs. Newton?" Ashley stepped forward and shook his hand. "Delighted to finally meet you in person. Shall we?"

He held the door open for all of us and gave us a chance to have a cursory glance around the room before throwing facts at us. Well, throwing them at Ashley mainly since he rightly assumed she was the leader of our search party.

I wasn't entirely sure what we were looking for but for me, this was looking pretty good. The place was actually a bit of a TARDIS, a lot bigger than the outside suggested. We were essentially looking for a blank canvas that we could build our vision on and this was as blank a canvas as they came. Whether the letting agent had done it to tidy things up or if the café really had been that boring, all the walls were a generic beige colour and the floors were an equally generic grey laminate. Needless to say, this was not the colour scheme we had been planning on.

"As you can see, the landlord has kept on top of all the maintenance and cleaning, so none of that would be required if you choose the property. I can show you the -."

"Actually Don," Ashley cut across, "could you give us a few minutes to have a look around first and then we can come back to you with any questions we might have. Thanks"

We all knew Ashley meant that as an order rather than a question from her no-nonsense tone and she didn't even wait for an answer from the Letting Agent before walking through the doors to the back rooms. Lucy gave me a confused look before we both decided to follow her, leaving Don by the front door, all by himself.

"Space out there is definitely a good size for a shop space though it's going to need a complete facelift," Ashley said offhandedly as she poked her head behind one of the closed doors before moving onto the other.

"So what's behind door number one?" Lucy asked with a grin.

"Office," Ashley replied pointing at the door to her left. "And this one as yours and Elsie's sewing room. What do you think?"

"Oh. So you want our input in this?" I joked, as I looked into the left-hand door. It was basically a box room that we could squeeze a desk and a couple of filing cabinets for all the boring stuff. "Can we paint it a brighter colour than moss-green?"

"Absolutely," Ashley said, a smile breaking her professional mask.

"Can I see my sewing room?" Lucy asked as Ashley stepped aside for her.

I squeezed in too to put my two cents in. It was the bigger of the two rooms and would be more than suitable for our purpose. As we really wanted to give Lucy a chance to pursue her sewing, since this was her dream after all, we had come up with the idea that one of the arms of the business we would push a lot would be the handmade vintage replica clothes and we were also offering the service of alterations. With John's help, we were also looking to sell these clothes through the website to widen our market.

We had a backup plan that we could run this out of Gran's house by taking orders in the shop and allowing Lucy work from there, especially since Gran was resolute that she wanted to help with the sewing side too. She was still refusing to be made an official employee and to get paid though since she was apparently doing it for the love of it. If we could have a room on the premises for consultations and fittings, it would make things look a little more professional.

"So far so good," Lucy said approvingly. "I'm liking what I'm seeing."

"There's still the last bit to see," Ashley pointed out as we followed her back into the front of the shop, giving Don a brief look of acknowledgement, then through the other door to what would be our tea room.

Casting my eye around the smaller room, I nodded. "It's not bad. Counter might be a bit too big for our needs if we're only doing tea, cake and sandwiches. Maybe we could get rid of some of it and it'll let us get another table or two in?"

Ashley grabbed a notebook out of her bag and began making notes. "Ryan will have no trouble doing that. I'm wondering whether we should just ask him to whip up a whole new counter because this one of a bit too metal-ly for my taste. If we get something wooden in, we can shabby chic it up and it'll fit the tone of the place. He's offered to do the tables and chairs for us if we want too. Apparently he can get those together quite quickly."

"He'll accept payment for them, right?" I asked, a twinge of guilt niggling at me at how much Ryan was offering to take on.

"Don't worry, he'll accept payment but I get wife's discount," she added with a smile. "Anything else?"

"How would you feel about knocking that wall down and making it one big room? People might be more inclined to have a drink if they can see it and people might be more willing to buy something if it keeps cropping up into their eye line."

"I can't see it being a problem for customers to throw it all together. Maybe we could get one of those old dressing screens and break the room up a bit so the tea room isn't right in their faces."

"Good idea," Ashley said, pointing at me with her pen before jotting down more notes. "I'll check that the landlord would be ok with us knocking the wall down, but if it means we're more likely to take the place, I think he'll agree. But all the changes are cosmetic which is what we were expecting anyway, so that's good news. Let's check out the kitchen and hope there's no nasty surprises to ruin our opinions."

Stepping behind the counter, we made our way into the kitchen which was more than suitable for our basic needs and it all looked pretty clean and well-kept. Hopefully looks weren't deceiving because then we could avoid delving into our budget to shell out for a new fridge for the time being.

"Ok, I've held on for as long as I can," Lucy said, levelling her eyes on me as she crossed her arms. "You owe me an explanation missus. What, where, when and how?"

Straight away I knew what she was on about.

"Don't you want to look over the state of the kitchen since that's kind of why we're here?" I looked beseechingly over at Ashley for help but I was getting nothing there.

"The sooner you tell us, the sooner we can get on with the job at hand," she shrugged.

"Fine!" I relented now it was two against one. "You know that evening I had to work the back-to-back shifts? Well, it happened then."

"What happened? Details woman! Did my brother make a move on you at work? Honestly, I never thought he had it in him."

"Nope." I felt my cheeks redden with embarrassment. "I was at his flat."

Lucy's eyebrows shot up so high, they were at risk of merging with her hair line. "His flat? What were you doing at his flat? Was this some kind of pre-arranged thing?"

"No! Not at all. I drove him home because it was raining and then, when he found out I hadn't eaten all through my double-shift, he made me go inside so he could make me something to eat. One second we're eating cheese on toast, the next he accidentally tells me he fancies me and it all sort of happened"

"Jessica Crawford, you dark horse. You slept with him, didn't you?" Ashley asked with a huge grin.

In response to that question, Lucy made a weird strangled sound. "This is such a horrible catch twenty-two. You're my friend and I want to know all the dirty details but those details involve my brother and I don't need those kind of mental images."

It served her right really since she pushed me into telling her but before I could torment her any more, Don popped his head back in the kitchen and asked how we were getting on. Thankfully Ashley immediately took control and started asking him about the ages of the kitchen equipment.

"Luce," I said quietly, "just so you know, your brother has been a perfect gentleman this whole time. He treats me really well and I really, *really* like him."

Lucy's blinding smile dazzled me. "Thanks for telling me. I knew you two would work well together. And, for the record, I know he's really into you too and I can already see how much happier he is because of you."

I should have left it there at Lucy's lovely words but I just couldn't resist adding a little more. "And he's *really* good in bed."

She made that weird sound again before hitting me in the arm and we then both burst into laughter, struggling to get ourselves under control, even when Don was looking over Ashley's shoulder at us. To try and calm ourselves, we started looking at all the shiny kitchen surfaces, not really sure what we were supposed to be looking for.

"Did you want to discuss it with your business partners?" we heard Don say and fixed our faces back into something that hopefully resembled a serious businesswoman.

"It's perfect," Ashley whispered as we huddled round her. "I don't think we're going to get premises so ready made at a better rate."

We all looked at each other, trying not to convey how we were actually feeling in front of the Letting Agent in case he decided to jack the price up if he knew we were too eager. Both Lucy and I gave a small nod to Ashley who immediately put her business face back on.

"Don, I think we need to sit down to discuss terms."

Shit just got real.

Chapter 19

Now we actually had premises, everything suddenly became a lot more terrifying. It was one thing to have an idea set out on pieces of paper and on spreadsheets, but it was another entirely to have to start putting things together officially. The three of us were now spending an inordinate amount of time at the table in Gran's kitchen, which Ashley had christened Vintage HQ. All three of us were working at full capacity and we'd roped in our nearest and dearest to put in almost as much effort too.

We had predicted that we could have an official opening in three months, which sounded like a lot of time but once we started writing down everything that needed doing, we realised we weren't being very generous after all. The shop still needed sprucing up but Ryan was able to do this in between his actual job and had been good enough to call in favours from a couple of friends with trade skills to help update the plumbing and electrics, as well as knocking down a wall, which was saving us a lot of money.

We were all itching to get into our shop to start decorating it, having spent a lot of time going over how we wanted it decorated. We had clashed a few times but eventually settled on compromises, which made me feel confident that we would be able to work together well to make the shop a success. But we couldn't make a start on that until Ryan and his friends had finished their work, so we forced ourselves to deal with the boring side of it all, since that was probably more important than decorating. Dividing the jobs between us equally, we dealt with HMRC and the council, we applied for the various licenses we needed to be able to serve tea and cakes and we took out insurance. All the boring stuff.

One of our other issues with opening in three months meant we were very close to Ashley's due date. We tried to suggest that we delay the opening until after the baby was born and she'd had a couple of months to recover and get settled but she wouldn't hear of it. She was certain she was going to be able to do everything and I knew that if anyone could pull off being a great mum and a successful entrepreneur, it was going to be Ashley. She said she would rather open the shop just before the baby arrived as it would take her mind of actually having to give birth and then hopefully things would run smoothly while she was resting up with the baby until she was ready to jump back in.

The three of us were gathered at Vintage HQ with a plate of chocolate brownies Gran had made that morning for us, trying to discuss a marketing strategy, which we were obviously putting Ashley in charge of.

"Do you think we can get the local paper to do a piece on us just before the opening?" Ashley asked, tapping away at her iPad. "Publicity is going to be our best friend going forward."

"I don't see why not. But on the safe side, we should probably send Lucy in to talk to them in person," I suggested.

"Why me?"

"Because the paper's editor is a middle-aged man, based on my research, and if we send you in a tight enough dress, you can probably make all kinds of demands."

"Well done for setting the feminist movement back about fifty years Jess. Why don't you do it instead?"

"Needs must," I shrugged. "And it won't work if I do it. I could flash my boobs at him and I still wouldn't get an inch of column space, since they're not that impressive."

"I hate to disagree with you, but *I* find them impressive."

I swivelled in my seat at the sound of the new voice in the kitchen, "Rob! How did you get in here?"

"Your Gran let me in."

My instant elation at seeing him dimmed as I looked past his shoulder for Gran, feeling more than a little mortified that she might have overheard his comment.

"Don't worry, she's still gardening out the front," he said, guessing where my embarrassment was coming from. "I'm too much of a gentleman to say something like that in front of your grandmother."

Lucy snorted at his comment. "What are you doing here Rob? Or have you just come to perve over your girlfriend> Because we're a bit too busy for that at the moment. It's all-hands-on-deck time."

"I know that dear sister, which is why I'm here." He held up a carrier bag as proof that he had another reason for being here. "You ladies have been working so hard, I thought you could probably do with some sustenance to keep you going."

"You're here to cook for us?" Lucy asked with incredulity.

"Oh Luce, give the poor man a break. I'm eating everything in sight at the moment, so I'll happily accept free food. What's on the menu Rob?" Ashley asked, barely looking up from her iPad.

"*Mozzarella in Carrozza* or mozzarella carriages if you want it in English translation," he replied with a pointed look at his sister. "That ok with you Lucia?"

A torn look crossed Lucy's face but eventually she relented. "Fine. Just try not to get in the way. We're really busy here."

But Rob just laughed to himself as he walked over to the worktop and started unpacking his bag. I gave my friends a quick apologetic look then scraped back my chair and went to join him.

"Did you really just come here to make us food?" I asked quietly, pressing up against his side.

"Nope. I actually did come here to perve on you. The food is just a good alibi. Where does your grandmother keep the frying pans?"

I pointed at the cupboard by his legs and enjoyed the view as he bent down but then forced myself back to my work since he actually was making food for us.

"Ok, we're halfway through the checklist which is good going," Ashley announced as she ticked a task off the list she had put together. "And that's most of the crap jobs done too. Next big thing to sort out is the website and the social media pages. Plus, we need to determine who wants to update and be in charge of this area. Luce, is John still happy to do the website for free?"

"Of course. He knows if he doesn't then he doesn't get any. If he does a good job then he gets the good stuff," she said with a knowing smile. What made her comment even better was the weird noise Rob made from his area of the kitchen. Apparently he didn't need to know that about his sister's private life.

"Well done Luce. So, we'll start basic with the website and gradually up it once we've found our footing with the shop, doing online orders too. Then social media, we stick to the basic three; Facebook, Twitter and Instagram?"

"Sounds good to me. We can link it so all three get updated with the same thing, which will at least save us a bit of time and hassle. I'll take social media if you want?" I offered and there was a nod from the other two at the table. "I'm thinking we post pictures of stock we have and hopefully, we can get customers to tag themselves in pictures of something they've bought. Maybe run a promo each month for the best outfit if we decide on a hashtag and give them a voucher to use in store? Then we can also upload pictures of Hollywood starlets from the fifties for inspiration."

"Perfect. This one is definitely yours Jess since you obviously have it sussed."

And that was how we continued, throwing ideas back and forth to each other, until the smell from the frying pan became too much for us.

"Are they ready yet Rob? I have an unborn child that needs feeding."

Carrying a plate loaded with cheesy-goodness, Rob set it down in the centre of the table with a flourish. "All yours ladies."

"What are they exactly?" I asked, grabbing one, knowing I was going to eat it anyway.

"Basically comfort food. It's mozzarella stuffed in white bread then fried in bread crumbs. Everything that's bad for you but so delicious," Lucy said with a moan as she took a bite. "*Molto buono.*"

I took a bite and let out my own groan as all that calorific goodness hit my taste buds. "Why have you never made this for me before?" But instead of answering, he just grinned and took a mouthful from his own carriage.

"Rob, it's two in the afternoon on a Wednesday," Lucy pointed out. "Why aren't you at work?"

"Leo's covering the kitchen. I've actually been thinking of giving him more responsibility and hiring a new assistant chef. This way I can cut back my hours so I'm not cooking every afternoon and every evening."

Lucy simply stared at him for a moment with wide eyes before scraping her chair back, walking around the table to him and placing her hand on his forehead.

"Luce, what the hell are you doing?"

"You don't feel feverish. How have you been feeling otherwise?"

"What's your point?" he asked impatiently.

"You just said you were going to cut your hours back at work. You're going to pass some duties onto Leo. You're clearly ill because you've never taken time off from work and you're a control freak who likes to be in charge of everything. Why else would you suggest cutting back your hours if you weren't sick? Did something heavy fall on your head on the way here? Have you been abducted by aliens recently?"

She went to feel his forehead again but he batted her hand away. "Oh Luce, you're really hilarious. I'm allowed to change things if I want to. The restaurant is comfortable so Leo can handle some shifts on his own. I don't want to spend all my waking hours there now I don't have to."

Lucy tilted her head and looked at him with narrowed eyes. "You've never been bothered about not having a life before. Why would...Oh! This is because of Jess!"

"What?" Panic flared in my chest that I was going to get blamed for something here. "I never told him to cut his hours down!"

"No, no, no," Lucy said quickly. "Not like that. I mean, he actually wants to spend time with you so he's willing to cut back his time at the restaurant since that was basically his life before you. I'm right, aren't I Rob?"

"Are you always going to be around to suck all the romance out of our relationship?" He sighed heavily before turning to me, thankfully looking less annoyed when his back was to his sister. "But she's right. Going forward, there's no way I'd be able to work every day and see you as much as I want to, especially when you're going to have your own business to deal with too, so I need to cut back. I'd rather spend my time with you."

I was about to answer when both Ashley and Lucy made a simultaneous *awwww* noise and I rolled my eyes instead. "Can I make one request?"

"Sure."

"When we spend all this time together, can we make sure these two numpties aren't around?"

"Deal," he grinned at me.

Chapter 20

Cutting his time back at the restaurant was the perfect idea because otherwise, I had no idea when I was going to see Rob and I really wanted to make this work. Since things with the shop were moving at breakneck speed, I was cutting my own hours back at the restaurant and the plan was for me to finish completely in a couple of weeks. Rob had hired a new waitress who was learning the ropes, along with a new assistant chef, so my dip in hours wouldn't have a tiring effect on everyone else.

Everything in my life was going so perfectly. I was so unused to that feeling and was waiting for something to go wrong. Great friends? Check. Gorgeous boyfriend who could cook like a dream? Check. Starting my own business? Check.

When I accidentally voiced my concerns to Gran over dinner that something was bound to go wrong because my run of good luck couldn't possibly last, she went straight into grandmother mode and told me not to be so stupid.

"You have good friends because you're a lovely, interesting person which is the same reason you have that young man of yours. He would be an idiot not to realise what a catch you are and is lucky to have *you*. As for your business, well, that speaks for itself. You clearly know what you're doing and that is why it's going to be a success. Look at all the great ideas you've already had. And, most importantly, you're willing to work hard. Luck isn't real, it's just some excuse lazy people use when things aren't going right; and you're certainly not a lazy person Jessica."

I half felt like I'd been told off for something in there but she had also put me at ease and I needed to stop doubting myself. "You're right, thanks Gran."

"If I ever get my hands on that Liam, I'll certainly give him a piece of my mind. I really don't like how much he knocked your confidence."

With my fork halfway to my mouth, I froze and stared at my grandmother. The first shock was the anger in her voice and the second shock came when I started to process what she had said. Had Liam really had that much of a lasting effect on me? I suppose he drained my confidence away in the end. When I had no work life to channel myself into, I put more into my relationship only for it to blow up in my face. Now, despite knowing how much Rob cared for me, there was always a voice at the back of my brain making me doubt I would be enough for him and soon he would just decide I wasn't for him.

Never mind Gran, if I ever got hold of Liam again I'd be giving him a piece of my own mind. I wasn't that person and had never doubted myself before he came along.

"But enough about that Liam," Gran said, the distaste obvious when she said his name, "Since you're courting with that new young man anyway. Though I still haven't had had a chance to properly speak with him. Invite him round for lunch on Sunday!"

"Why? So you can interrogate him?" I laughed.

"No. I'd just like to get to know him since I have the feeling he might be around for a while. He's Lucy's brother after all so I don't feel the need to question his character. I'll leave it with you to arrange for him to come round for Sunday lunch."

Nodding, I agreed and sent him a message after dinner saying his presence was requested for Sunday lunch. I received confirmation back later that evening when he had finished at the restaurant saying he'd be there.

So, a couple of a days later, Roberto Amato was on my grandmother's doorstep for a Sunday roast, two bunches of sunflowers and a bottle of red wine in hand. It was comforting to see he looked a little nervous.

"I bought you these because I'm sure I remembered you saying they were your favourite at some point. And it seemed a safe bet to bring your gran the same."

I couldn't even remember telling him I loved sunflowers but he'd actually retained that tiny piece of information. I gave him the type of kiss I probably couldn't give him in front of my grandmother to say thank you before leading him through to the kitchen.

"Rob, they're lovely, thank you." Gran said when she accepted her own bunch with a delighted smile. "Lunch won't be much longer. I thought while the sun was out, we could eat in the garden."

Agreeing that it was a great idea, I grabbed one of the spare table cloths from the airing cupboard and Rob started to collect up plates and cutlery, which would immediately win him Brownie points with Gran.

"Stop worrying. You're doing well," I said as I unfurled the table cloth over the table on the patio.

"I didn't realise it was that noticeable," Rob admitted as he smoothed out the fabric on his side of the table.

"I wasn't aware you were even capable of being nervous," I teased.

"Not normally but apparently you're the exception to that rule." The idea of that pleased me immensely. "I know how important your grandmother is to you, so it's really important she likes me."

"Is that an Italian thing?" I joked.

"It's a good boyfriend thing," he grinned.

Well, he had nothing to worry about in that department. If there was an Olympics for boyfriends, he was basically the Usain Bolt.

Just as he finished laying the cutlery with restaurant level precision, Gran stepped out the back door carrying a serving dish filled with potatoes and fluffy Yorkshire puddings. As soon as the smell hit me, I began to salivate.

"Can I help you carry anything out Mrs Crawford?" Rob asked quickly.

"Thank you Rob. If you could grab the dish of vegetables, that would be wonderful. And call me Elsie."

I caught his eye before he headed inside and winked. Gran telling Rob that he could call her Elsie meant that already liked him.

Gran herself went back inside to bring out the beef joint she'd been cooking all afternoon and set it in the centre of the table. As she began to slice it and Rob filled the glasses with wine, I helped myself to the roast potatoes and began piling them onto my plate. Once I had a bit of everything on my plate I did my usual thing of drowning it all in gravy.

"Good job I made extra," Gran said with a smile as she watched me empty most of the gravy boat onto my plate.

"She knows exactly how I operate," I informed Rob.

"This looks absolutely delicious," he said to Gran, making her smile with pride. "Buon appetito."

I echoed him before get stuck into my lunch, going straight for the potatoes. "Oh Gran, you've done it again. Your roast potatoes are always so on point."

"There's a great crispiness to them," Rob agreed as he cut through one to demonstrate his point like a Masterchef judge. "What do you use on them?"

"Goose fat. And it helps the potatoes are home grown. Home grown food always tastes better. I think it's the satisfaction factor," Gran said proudly as she gestured towards her vegetable patch at the bottom of the garden.

From that moment on, they bonded over foodie talk whilst I happily just ate my meal in silence as they compared recipes and cooking tips.

"Elsie, that was absolutely delicious," Rob said as he mopped up the last of his gravy on his plate with a final mouthful of Yorkshire pudding.

"I hope you've saved room for dessert. It's nothing too filling, just a nice Eton Mess."

"Homemade strawberries?" he asked.

"Of course."

He then flashed her a smile oozing with that Italian charm no woman, no matter her age, could shield herself from.

If only he'd been that way when we'd first met.

On second thoughts, it was probably better that he wasn't.

As Gran made to stand and clear away the plates, I gestured for her to sit back down so I could do it.

Having done nothing to help so far, I should probably start pulling my weight.

I managed to get everything back inside in just two trips from the table to the kitchen thanks to my fantastic waitressing skills, and when I carried the Eton Mess out, Rob was already filling up Gran's glass with more wine as he talked her through a family recipe for lemon chicken.

By the time we finished, the sky was beginning to turn pink and the temperature had dropped to the point where we couldn't ignore it any longer and probably should look to head inside. But it was safe to say that the meal had been a complete success. Gran was completely in love with Rob, not that he'd ever had anything to worry about.

"Jess," Gran started as I began folding the table cloth away as Rob balanced the empty dessert bowls and wine glasses in his hands, "had you thought to invite Rob to your parents' party in a couple of weeks' time?"

I managed to peek a sly look at Gran as I made my final fold on the table cloth. "You know what Gran, I'd completely forgotten all about that. Thanks for reminding me."

I obviously hadn't forgotten but knew it was best to wait until Gran had given her full approval on Rob. Although I couldn't see him abandoning the restaurant for a whole weekend so I wasn't entirely sure I should even mention it. It was a big ask for such an early stage in our relationship.

Rob raised a questioning eyebrow at me but I whispered that I would fill him in on the way out to the car. I let him say his goodbyes to Gran, who made him promise he would come round again for another lunch. He even offered to do the cooking which probably made Gran love him even more…if that were possible.

"So, this party?" he asked once we were out of the door and I was walking him to his car, even though it was parked next to the Volvo in the driveway.

I leaned myself against the bonnet of his car. "It's my parent's thirtieth wedding anniversary the weekend after next and they've decided to throw a big party to celebrate. Did you fancy being my plus one?"

My parents had only returned from their big adventure at the beginning of the week but it seemed, based on the phone calls I'd had from them, that they'd found a whole new lease of life. Apparently Mum had even become interested in yoga and Buddhism after they had picked an option to spend a week staying at a monastery in Thailand. They went in for the experience and Mum came out converted, with a new appreciation for the world. She'd talked Dad into having a big gathering for their anniversary so they could celebrate with friends and family, even if it was to be done at such short notice.

They'd tried to fill me in the best they could on their trip but there was just so much to it that I wouldn't get the full effect until I saw them in person again. Though I could hear the excitement and wonder in both their voices as they tried to tell me over the phone. It was obvious they'd had an amazing time.

I'd managed to briefly fill them in on what was happening in my life too and they seemed incredibly pleased with my decision to start up my own business and Mum especially was interested to hear that I had a new man in my life, so had told me to extend him an invite too.

"Will it be in Oxford?" he asked, his face falling a little.

"Just outside of." I rested my hands on his shoulders. "Don't worry. I know you're not going to be able to leave the restaurant for a whole weekend. It's short notice to spring this on you; I'm perfectly aware of that."

"I just don't think I could leave Leo in charge for the whole..."

I cut him off with a brief kiss. "Don't feel guilty. I understand."

But he still looked guilty which made me smile.

"I'll arrange something for another weekend, I promise. I'll win your parents over as well as I won your Gran over."

I had no doubt that he would do just that.

Chapter 21

"Ow! Gran! If you keep doing that, I'll have no hair left."

"Nonsense Jess. This is the only way to get the height so it holds properly. This was how we did it my day."

I was sat at the dressing table in my old room at my parents' house that still looked exactly the same as it had when I'd moved out, despite my parents' claims they were going to redecorate and turn it into some kind of study-slash-relaxation room. I'm sure one day they would finally get around to it.

I'd driven down with Gran the evening before so we didn't have to rush and so I could catch up with my parents. Being more academically inclined, they were the type of people who were very intelligent but lacked any common sense or know how about everyday things. Since they were both rather old school and had only just learned how to text properly, FaceTime chats never went well, so we normally had to talk over the landline. I'd obviously mentioned the shop on our chats but telling them the plans face-to-face made it all the more special. Over dinner, I'd been able to see how visibly proud they were of me and it felt wonderful to be able to tell them how positive my life was finally.

Plus, they had a million photos from their trip that they had wanted to show off.

It was odd, but the last time I'd seen my parents in person had been after Grandad's funeral quite a few months before, mostly because of their impromptu decision to go travelling, and so much had changed in that time. Thankfully Dad was much more like his old self. With both him and Mum still sporting envious tans, they looked refreshed and ten years younger. You couldn't quite believe they were celebrating thirty years of marriage.

They were holding their party at the events venue on the grounds of an old manor house in Banbury and it looked like the weather was on our side since the venue had the loveliest gardens and Gran not being able to take a walk around them would have been a shame.

As it was such a special occasion, I was required to dress up, which meant a Gran original from the fifties again. She'd basically made the choice for me and gave me a pale blue dress that would apparently bring out my eyes. This I was incredibly grateful for. But she'd also insisted I'd wear heels and had dug out a pair of white kitten heels from somewhere. These I was not so grateful for because, even though they weren't exactly high, I was probably going to stack in them.

When I had emerged from the bathroom in my dress, Gran had exclaimed that I looked like a blonde Audrey Hepburn. I wasn't convinced I had the face for that kind of comparison but the dress certainly made me feel that way. It was very much in the style of what I'd seen her wearing, modestly covering me up to my clavicle but baring most of my shoulders while showing off my waist before the swishy skirt flared out, ending at my knees. In these dresses, I never felt like I was missing anything. While it was true they highlighted my less-than-voluptuous figure, they made me feel more feminine than anything else I'd ever worn. I can't believe it had taken me so long to appoint my grandmother as my personal stylist.

But it was that comparison that led me to be sat at the dressing table and Gran backcombed the life out of my hair in an attempt to create an Audrey-esque beehive. Even though I had no idea how I was going to take it down and get my hair back to normal, I had to admit that it looked really good.

My point was confirmed when I headed downstairs and ran into my mother.

"Jess, you look so beautiful. And so grown up. Thirty years of marriage and an adult daughter. I'm reminded just how old I'm getting."

"Well you definitely don't look it Mum."

That was the truth. Dressed in a floral skirt and a simple white blouse, my mum looked wonderful. Whilst I knew she dyed her hair to her original brown, her face still had a youthful glow to it that made her look years younger. Especially now she had discovered yoga on her travels and adopted that whole zen outlook on life.

"Are we ready to go? I think I heard the taxi beep outside."

Dad came down the stairs, clapping his hands together eagerly. Dressed in his "good suit", he looked years younger too, though he hadn't really jumped onto the yoga idea and all the Buddhist teachings like Mum had. I think it was just because he was so happy.

We jumped in the waiting taxi that took us to Lockton Hall. Dad was adamant that since this was a celebration, no one should worry about driving getting in the way of a good drink and had arranged the taxi for both ways.

As we headed up the long, gravelled driveway, I pressed my nose to the window to get a good look at Lockton Hall, which didn't disappoint. The imposing Tudor manor was as impressive as I had expected. But the taxi turned off just before we reached the house, veering off to the side to take us to their events venue which were the converted stables.

Not that that was any less impressive.

The venue was small enough to be intimate but big enough that it didn't feel cramped with all the tables set out and looked beautifully historic having kept a lot of its original features. Mum and Dad were expecting about sixty people to help them celebrate and the plan was to start at 3pm and carry on until midnight.

People started to arrive just before three and I began chatting to some cousins I hadn't seen for a while, helping myself to a glass of Buck's Fizz and whatever canopy was thrown under my nose while we all milled about on the lawn in front of the stables, enjoying the warm weather. There was also a giant chess set and a croquet game set up to keep the children, and a lot of adults, amused.

"Jess, have you seen the photographs yet?" Gran asked before taking another sip of prosecco.

She was already on her second glass which made me smile, since Gran wasn't exactly a drinker, but she seemed to be enjoying herself. She also had no problem walking across grass in her own heels after having alcohol, unlike me. And I didn't really have the alcohol excuse to use either.

"No, not yet."

Mum had mentioned that she'd put together a collection of photographs for the occasion but she'd brought the boards to the venue a few days before, so I hadn't had a chance to see what she'd done.

I had a quick look down at my watch. "If I go check them out now, I can be right in prime position for when the buffet opens at four. Don't drink too much Gran," I added with a grin.

Her response was to swat me in the arm and tell me to respect my elders.

I made my way across the lawn and back into the stables, occasionally having to stop and say a quick hello to someone who remembered me more than I remembered them. Eventually I was able to cross the room to check out the boards. The first was filled with pictures of my parents in the early days, looking so young and happy. The second featured people who I recognised more; my parents' when they were officially my parents. I even featured in a few of these photos in the mix of family trips, Christmases, birthdays and just general family life. Some of these photos evoked a warm rush of memories for me, reminding me how much I had lucked out in life, while a couple were so embarrassing, I had mentally repressed those times and the outfits I had been dressed in and would be having serious words with my mum for reminding me that I tragically had a mullet when I was five years old.

The third board was the one that was completely new to me. It was my parents as they were in current time, living life to the full as they travelled their way across Asia. Even though I had already heard all the stories of their adventures the night before and been through the pictures, I was just enjoying seeing the smiling faces of my parents.

While I was busy basking in the warm feelings being home was bringing my way, a figure moved next to me, peering at the photographs.

"Hi Jess."

The familiar voice immediately dampened my happiness and I felt my stomach tighten.

"Hi Liam," I said on complete auto-pilot, shifting my body so I was now face-to-face with my ex-boyfriend for the first time since our break up.

"You look amazing."

"Erm, thanks."

I shuffled awkwardly on my heels, not knowing if I should turn around or be polite and strike up a conversation. I was completely unprepared. I hadn't even considered the slight possibility that he would even be here, even though I knew full well that his parents would be as they were still very good friends with mine.

But instead of running away like the old Jess would have done, I faced my problems head on. "How are you?"

I assumed he was ok as he looked exactly like the man I had left four months before. Even in the vicinity of his home town, he still looked like London Liam, so much so that I couldn't even picture the man I had originally fallen in love with.

"I'm not too bad. Work's been crazy so that it's all I've been doing at the moment."

He looked at me with a flash of unease, as if he were expecting me to ask about Lara, but the truth was, I didn't care in the slightest. Without even realising, I was completely over all of that because I had actually moved onto bigger and better things.

"I think, sorry, I *know*, I owe you an apology. Would it be alright to go outside so we can talk about things? It won't take long," he added quickly.

I was curious to hear what he had to say more than anything else, since things had ended so abruptly. Not that I regretted the way I went about it at all. But after everything my mum had said about the yogi teachings she came across on her adventures, it might be good for my soul to hear him out and forgive him.

"Sure. I reckon I can spare five minutes."

"Really?" He smiled with obvious relief and I saw a glimpse of old Liam. Maybe he wasn't completely gone after all. "I promise we'll be back before speeches."

The cynical voice at the back of my brain whispered that a promise from him didn't exactly mean a lot, but I managed to silence it as I followed him out of the venue and we began walking across the perfectly manicured lawn.

"I know it probably isn't enough," he said after a minute walking in silence, "but I really am sorry. I'm not even sure why I did it, which isn't an excuse, and I am sorry I hurt you."

"Apology accepted," I said lightly, feeling surprisingly better now he'd actually admitted to what he'd done. "It's all in the past."

"That still doesn't make up for the fact I acted like a complete dick."

"No it doesn't," I agreed. "But it did show me how wrong for each other we'd become. Though I wish I hadn't come to that realisation in quite that fashion."

He stayed silent as we walked onto the little wooden bridge that ran over the stream and he rested his arms on the barrier, watching a family of ducks on the water.

"I think you're probably right about us. So, where's life taken you now? I heard you went to live with your grandmother."

"She didn't really give me much of a choice," I laughed. "But it turns out it was one of the best decisions I ever made. Apparently everything I needed was in Pickney all along."

"I'm glad. Are you seeing someone then?"

It seemed like an odd thing to discuss with my cheating ex-boyfriend but I was such a different person now, and so detached from old Jess' life, that the awkwardness barely registered.

"I am. A really great guy who has his own restaurant. It's a funny story actually because he's the brother of my new business partner. I met Lucy first, she started coming to the sewing bee I helped set up and then got me a job with Rob while I decided what to do with my life. I was sure he hated me but apparently not."

Liam stood up straight now and was practically gawping at me. Maybe I had jumped the comfortable level a little too quickly. Or maybe it was just a funny story if you were the people involved.

"Did you say business partner?" he asked eventually.

That was the thing he picked up from all of that?

"I did," I replied defensively, not entirely comfortable with the judgement in his tone. "I'm setting up my own business with two other friends."

"Really? And what's the business?" I didn't entirely like the odd smirk he was giving me either.

"A vintage shop."

That smirk went straight into a condescending grin that made my blood boil. "A vintage shop? Seriously? Come on Jess, is this really going to be a good idea because it sounds like a disaster waiting to happen."

"Excuse me? And why would it be a disaster? We've planned everything down to the smallest detail and all the numbers we've run predict that we're going to do well with it."

"Yeah but what do you really know about running a business? Look at how bad your working life was before this. You couldn't even hold down a simple admin job."

What the actual -?

"If you recall, I actually had a good job here, that I was great at," I said, fighting to keep a lid on my anger. "I then gave that job up because you asked me to move to London with you and that was when everything went downhill."

"It's not my fault your work life suffered." He held his hands up defensively. "Or that no one wanted to hire you. Maybe you were just aiming to high. It was then all our trouble started too. If you'd just gone for something more your level, we might not have drifted apart from the tension it caused."

And that was it. That was the negative voice at the back of my head that had made me doubt myself so much over the last couple of years. It was never my voice but Liam's, with his little digs here and there that gradually knocked away at my confidence. Gran had been right.

"You know what Liam, I honestly don't care what you think and I *will* be making this business a success. And one more thing…"

I'm not even sure where it came from, but all the anger I felt towards him balled itself into my fist and was released right in the centre of his face. As he bent over, holding his nose, I finally felt like I'd had my closure.

"Thanks for the apology, but you can shove it up your arse," I added before turning my back on him once and for all.

As I stormed back across the lawn to the party, trying to stop my heels making divots in the perfectly manicured lawn, I had a momentary lapse in concentration and one shoe flew off back behind me. I let out an audible huff as I had to bend down to retrieve it.

"Need a hand there Cinderella?"

I looked up and my mood levels practically shot through the roof – in the right direction this time. "Rob?"

He was walking across with the lawn with Gran, so I hobbled over to them, ignoring the lost shoe and rested my hands on Rob's shoulders, partly for balance and partly just as excuse to touch him. "What are you doing here?"

"It turns out he could make the party after all," Gran replied for him, beaming. "We headed out this way to see where you'd gotten to. What are you doing out here...and in just one shoe?"

"Don't even ask," I said wryly. "I got into an *altercation* with Liam."

"What?"

I felt Rob's shoulders tense beneath my hands and realised I had probably mentioned that little piece of information to the wrong person.

"It's fine," I said quickly, not liking the stern line of Rob's mouth. "He wanted to apologise for what happened but only ended up reminding me what a twat he is and how I'm so much better off without him."

"Really?" Rob still looked angry but his shoulders had relaxed, so that was something.

"Yes," I said forcefully, moving my hands behind his neck and locking eyes. "I lost all patience with him when he essentially told me it was my fault he cheated and if I started my own business, it was probably going to fail. I clouted him, told him where to go then walked away."

"You punched him?" Rob asked, all traces of anger leaving his face now. "That's my girl. Do you want me to call some old friends in Italy so we can arrange to have him *dealt with*? I'm sure someone out there will know someone who knows *someone*."

"That won't be necessary Rob," Gran cut in, staring ahead of her. "I believe I will deal with this myself. Excuse me."

Rob looked at me in confusion as Gran was already walking away from us. I turned to see Liam, who seemed to be planning to head back to the party himself until he was halted by my grandmother at her most formidable. The last thing we heard her say, in her best serious grandmother voice, was, "Excuse me young man. I think you and I need to have a chat."

As they walked further out of ear shot, I started to giggle, which eventually turned into a full on laugh, causing Rob to start laughing too.

"I don't think I've had the chance to tell you yet, but you look beautiful," he said once our laughter died away.

"Well it was about time you told me. But seriously, you left work to come here?"

I felt his hands lightly trail up and down the length of my body. "Yeah. Leo was more than happy to do the evening shift without me. I'm worried I've given him too much power too quickly. He's more ambitious than I gave him credit for."

"What changed your mind?" I asked calmly, though my heart was hammering against my chest.

"I was stood over the oven during the lunch prep when it hit me that my heritage is very into the whole family is important thing. So if I couldn't give up one afternoon to spend time with the family of the woman I love, then a whole country would probably be very disappointed in me."

"The woman you love?" I echoed.

"Yes, the woman I love," he said softly. "I thought I better come here to tell you that too. I had planned a better speech while I was driving here but I forgot most of it as soon as I saw you bent over, about to pick your shoe up."

He'd dropped everything for me and driven two hours across the country? I thought those kinds of gestures only existed in the movies. How could I not love a man who did that for me?

"You already said everything perfectly. And I love you too." I then allowed him to kiss me in that masterful way of his that made my legs turn to jelly. "I'm so glad you're here."

"Me too. I -."

He was cut off when his phone started its shrill ring. "It's Lucy. She shouldn't even know I'm here yet she still manages to ruin the moment. Hang on, let me get rid of her."

He answered his phone but I heard Lucy's muffled voice coming through the speaker straight away. Rob's eyebrows knitted together as he looked down at me. "I'm with her now Luce. Jess, do you have your phone on you?"

"No, I left my bag back at the venue."

"She doesn't have her phone Luce, that's why she hasn't replied. Ok, got it. We'll be right there." He slipped his phone back into his pocket before grabbing my hand. "Get your shoe. We need to go now."

Chapter 22

Once Rob explained the situation to me on our way back to the party so I could grab my stuff and say goodbye to my parents, I picked up the pace. Ashley had gone into labour almost seven weeks early and Lucy had received a phone call from a worried sounding Ryan, so she had headed straight for the hospital to hang around there in case there was anything she could do to help.

Gran was adamant I leave immediately saying she would make Dad drive her back in a couple of days, that she would bring my things and made me promise I would ring her as soon as I knew what the situation with Ashley was.

Thankfully the roads were clear and I noticed Rob was putting his foot down, risking a speeding ticket on quite a few occasions. He really was a wonderful man and I wanted to bask more in the knowledge that he had travelled all that way here because he loved me, but I was too concerned about Ashley to think about myself right now. Rob clearly sensed my distress and most of our journey was in silence, half-listening to the radio as background noise, though when the roads smoothed out, he did occasionally take a hand off the wheel to reach across and give my hand a quick squeeze.

I called Lucy when we were about an hour away to let her know we would be there soon.

"Any news?" Rob asked as soon as I disconnected the call.

"There's still nothing," I sighed. "I supposed no news is good news?"

We fell back into silence as Rob put his foot down a little more, getting us to the hospital in under an hour, pulling into the first parking space he came across in the car park.

Despite still having those blasted heels on, I practically sprinted into the hospital and up to the maternity ward, gripping at Rob's hand. Since I'd had no update from Lucy, I had no idea if Ashley was ok and what the situation was with the baby.

As soon as we turned onto the ward, I instantly spotted Lucy who was pacing nervously in front of the nurses' station while John was sat in one of the chairs, his foot tapping the floor restlessly.

Hurrying over to Lucy, my heels echoed on the polished floor which was enough to make my friend look over in my direction and pull me into a tight hug as soon as I reached her. Up close, Lucy's usually flawless face looked tired with worry but she had been here for at least three hours.

"What's the news?"

"I have no idea. She's refusing to tell me anything." Lucy aimed an annoyed look at the nurse manning the station.

"Hi. I'm sorry, you're probably very busy, but is there any chance you can tell us anything about Ashley Newton? Even if it's the smallest thing. We just want to know she's ok." If Lucy hadn't been able to get anything out of her then it was unlikely I would but it was worth a try.

"I'm sorry," the nurse replied briskly, barely looking up from her paperwork. "At this stage, we can only pass information on to family members."

"Oh these women are definitely classed as family," came a voice behind us.

Lucy and I whipped round so fast, it was surprising we hadn't created enough force to blow the paperwork off the desk. As soon as my eyes rested on a very happy looking Ryan, my heart left my throat and returned to its normal home.

"I'm a dad!" he practically shouted to the whole ward.

Unable to contain our excitement, we both threw ourselves at him for hugs and to offer our congratulations.

"How's Ash? Is she ok? She gave us quite the scare."

Shaking his head, Ryan started to chuckle. "You know Ashley, never one to do things the easy way. Though that might be the baby's fault so I guess I have two girls to keep me on my toes now."

"You have a daughter!" Lucy cried, clapping her hands together. "Oh my god, you have a daughter."

"Yep. Don't know how I got so lucky to be surrounded by beautiful women," he shrugged, the smile refusing to leave his face. "Sorry we left you out here for so long but I just couldn't tear myself away. They're both settled now and I know Ash is dying to see you."

Ryan started accepting congratulations from John and Rob as we headed in the direction of Ashley's room now we had been granted access through the doors. Dousing ourselves in the alcohol gel before knocking on her door, we slowly popped our heads around.

"Well don't just stand there gawping. Come in!" Ashley said from her position in bed, a tiny pink bundle in her arms. Though her bob looked less sleek than usual with the fringe plastered to her forehead due to her exertions and she was obviously tired, at that moment, I didn't think there was a woman in the world who looked more beautiful than Ash did. She was practically radiating happiness, as if she was being lit from the inside. Motherhood was definitely going to agree with her and hopefully all her past concerns had melted away.

I wasn't sure if the baby was asleep or just quiet but I tried my best to walk on the balls of my feet to keep the heels from making their clicking noise. I finally reached the bed and my heart melted at the sight of a wrinkled little face poking out between the blanket and a matching pink hat. She was just so tiny.

"Ladies, allow me to introduce you to Amber Elsie Newton," Ashley said proudly. "I hope your gran won't mind that I've stolen her name."

"Of course not. She'll probably be over the moon," I replied, gently setting myself down on Ashley's bed as Lucy took the space on the other side.

"I'd always liked the idea of giving my child the name of a grandparent but I don't even remember mine and they weren't exactly around to make a positive impact on my life. Over the last few months, your gran has become the closest thing I've ever had to one."

"Oh stop, you're going to make me cry," I laughed as my eyes pricked with tears. "God knows how Gran will react to that story if I'm tearing up already."

"So what happened Ash?" Lucy asked, thankfully giving me a chance to compose myself. "When I got the call from Ryan saying he was at the hospital because you'd gone into early labour, he sounded terrified."

"It was all a bit scary," she admitted. "They made such a fuss about me because I'm early and that made me worry more, since I've never done this before but aside from the fact that the whole thing actually hurt like hell, we had no problems. She's a little smaller than she should be but otherwise completely healthy, which on the plus side, at least I didn't have to squeeze anything bigger out of me. Apparently she was just desperate to get out and finally meet everyone."

Three sets of eyes settled on the tiny bundle and we all fell silent as we watched her sleep, not a care in the world. All she had to do was move her tiny fist or make a soft snuffling sound and we were all smiling at each other like complete idiots. She was the most adorable thing I had ever seen in my life.

"I want one," Lucy eventually said wistfully, her eyes still fixed on Amber.

"Do it and we can be Yummy Mummies together. Then we can work on Jess."

"I don't think it would take much persuading to get Rob on board. From what I can tell, you guys are getting in a lot of practice already," Lucy said, adding a wink for the full effect.

"Don't even joke about it," I laughed.

Though at the back of my mind, I didn't completely hate the idea. Even though it was still early days, Rob was the only person I could picture myself doing all those grown-up things with. Maybe it was because I was finally becoming a real grown up and could start thinking about that or maybe it was simply because I had never felt the way I did about him like I had with anyone else.

But, just because I was open to the idea of having kids with him, didn't mean it was happening any time soon. Babies were a long, long way off.

"By the way Jess, why are you so dressed up? Not that I don't appreciate the effort for a hospital visit to see me."

Ashley's question brought me out of a slightly worrying thought tangent. I had been busy deciding which mix of mine and Rob's features would be the most adorable combination, settling on his dark hair and my blue eyes. But babies were still definitely a long, long, *long* way off.

"Deflate your ego, I didn't dress up for you. I was at my parents' anniversary thing today and Gran insisted I made an effort. That's why I'm in heels and my hair is shaped like a beehive."

"That was in Oxfordshire! I completely forgot you had that today."

"Well you kind of had other things to deal with," I grinned, glancing down at a still-sleeping Amber.

"But what are you doing here? Don't tell me you left the party for me?"

"Of course I did Ash. First of all, we weren't sure what sort of condition you were in so obviously I had to get here. But more importantly, I wanted to be here. My parents' have an anniversary every year but how often are you going to see your friend's new born for the first time? Why are you crying?"

"Pregnancy hormones," Ashley answered, trying to wipe away tears whilst not disturbing Amber.

Lucy grabbed a tissue from the box next to the bed and handed it to her. "Thanks. I just can't believe you both dropped everything for me to hang around the hospital. You know you two are more than friends to me? I think of you like sisters and not just sewing sisters but real sisters."

A quick glance at Lucy told me her eyes were welling up as much as mine, though I for one, couldn't blame it on pregnancy hormones.

"When I first found out I was pregnant, the one thing that kept worrying me more than anything else was that Amber wasn't going to be surrounded by family. Sure, she had me and Ryan but no crazy aunties or grandparents to spoil her and until I met you two, I didn't know anyone in Pickney and had no real friends. You have no idea what it means to me that my daughter will have you two to look up to when she's growing up. You honestly have no idea how much you've helped me since the day I met you."

"Stop it Ash," Lucy said through a stream of free-flowing tears. "What about what you two have done for me? If I'd never met you both, I wouldn't have been following my dream. I'd probably have gone back to being an accountant and be very unhappy right now."

"Seriously, both of you need to stop this and give yourselves some credit," I cut in, my voice cracking will all my feelings. "We all know how rubbish my life would have been if I hadn't met you both. I mean, you helped me out of my funk, gave me a social life again and gave me a career. I'd be nowhere without you two."

"How about," Ashley suggested through her tears, "we all agree to the fact that our lives would have been rubbish without each other and we all helped make each other the versions of ourselves we deserve to be?"

"Deal. I love you girls," Lucy said as she gestured for us all in for an awkward group hug where we tried not to squash the baby.

"Isn't it the baby who is supposed to be crying uncontrollably?"

All of us detangled from our group hug and looked over at Ryan, who now had John and Rob in tow. They had probably grown tired of waiting for us but the image of three women with tear stained faces might have made them wish they'd waited outside a little longer.

"We're having an emotional bonding session," Lucy informed them. "John, I think I want a baby."

Though I definitely saw a flicker of terror on John's face, he quickly composed himself and made the type of quip we were all expecting. "Distract the room and I'll grab this one for you. Anyway, we're trying to organise when we can take Ryan out to wet the baby's head. Ashley, when is he allowed out?"

Lucy rolled her eyes and made some comment about men being idiots as the idiot men in question made themselves comfortable and we all watched over Amber until she woke up with a little cry and Ashley said she needed feeding, which we knew was our time to go and give the new family some space.

The hospital wanted to keep Ashley in for a couple of days to monitor her, just as a precaution, so we said our goodbyes, promising to visit again tomorrow.

"When you come back, will you bring some of the shop stuff? We can run through things while I'm still bedbound."

"Really? You want to work?" I asked. "You have the perfect excuse to get out of it."

"I'm a working mum now Jess. Got to make every second count," she added with a smile.

As we left the ward, Lucy took hold of John's hand and started whispering something to him.

"Twenty-quid says we're back here in less than a year," I said quietly to Rob. "I can't imagine John saying no to Lucy when she wants something."

He slipped his arm around me and laughed. "I'm not stupid enough to bet on something that's almost a certainty. Not now anyway. Besides, I quite like the idea of being cool Uncle Rob."

I looked over at him, raising an eyebrow. "Really? You actually think you're going to be the cool one?"

One Month Later

"Do these look ok or do you think I should have put less out?"

The chalk paint was barely dry on the shabby chic chest of drawers Ryan had found time to whip up for us and we were ready to officially open Deja Vintage.

"No, the more the better," Ashley said, coming over to me, Amber cradled in her arms. "By that, I mean a better chance of selling things."

Our countdown clock had reached thirty minutes until we opened the doors on our new business, and our new future, and I was still faffing about the tiny little details. Like the vintage jewellery I was trying to artfully display on top of the drawers to tempt people into buying something.

"Wine delivery!"

My heart leapt in my chest as I turned to the now so familiar voice and Rob walked into the shop carrying a crate full of wine.

Even though it was a Saturday, he'd closed the restaurant for the day so he could properly support me and Lucy. And he'd donated a generous amount of wine for the occasion. Just another thing to add to the long list of reasons why I loved him.

"Wow. The place looks amazing," he said as he set his crate down and gave me a quick kiss on the cheek. "Last time I was here, the electrics were still exposed and Ryan had just finished ripping up the floors."

Ryan had been the only one allowed to see the progress of the shop, seeing as he was the one responsible for all the progress. Once the inside had had its facelift, Lucy and I had attacked it with paintbrushes while Ashley became our overseer, as she was technically supposed to be resting up. Following the inspiration of our Pinterest board, we had made the shop the epitome of shabby chic with white walls, hardwood floors and well-placed accents to create the desired effect.

Lucy had found a couple of armchairs at a car boot that, once spruced up a bit, were set to the side, with a small table in between which we'd scattered with old copies of Vogue from the 50s and 60s Gran had unearthed from her personal collections. The ones that we hadn't put on the table, we had removed the front overs of and framed them to sit on the walls alongside some black and white photographs of classic Hollywood starlets.

"Rob, either make yourself useful or get out the way," Lucy said as she bustled past him, an armful of vintage dresses she was planning to hang on the antique armour we had picked up cheap. Ryan had removed the doors on it so we could use as a quirky way of displaying our wears. She was wearing a cherry print halter dress of her own making and looked drop dead gorgeous in it. Lucia Amato was probably the best advert we could have.

"Lovely to see you too dearest sister," he replied sarcastically before turning back to me, "Where do you want these?"

"Over on the counter in the tea room." I gestured over at the dressing screen that was separating the main shop and the tea room. "Just follow the smell of freshly baked brownies."

As a way of drawing people in for our opening day, we were tempting them with glasses of wine and cakes, passing it off as celebrating our grand opening. Gran and Olive had made enough to cover every person in town coming in to see us.

The mood was at an all-time high as we all ran around, sorting out the little bits and pieces, anticipating the moment we could throw open the door and the dream finally became a reality.

"Did you feel like this just before your restaurant opened?" I asked Rob as he came back to my side of the shop after dealing with the wine. "All shaky from nervousness, but a good kind of nervousness that's coming from excitement?"

"I was so nervous I had to keep running back and forth to the toilet because I thought I was going to be sick," he admitted.

"No way!" I couldn't believe that Mr. Always-in-Control would have been that bad.

"Scariest thing I'd ever done. All I could think about was what would happen if it failed. What if it all went wrong."

"I never would have expected that from you. How long until you got over that feeling?"

"As soon as I turned the oven on for the first ever sitting," he laughed. "As soon as I started cooking, I was fine. I was where I wanted to be, doing what I wanted and all my hard work had paid off."

"I know it sounds really New Agey, but I kind of feel this is one of those pre-planned, written in the stars things. My life was never really going to kick off until I came to Pickney. Without coming here, I wouldn't be as happy as I am and have as much purpose as I do."

"Oh Jess, *la mia bella idiota*, you still don't see the bigger picture." Rob was looking at me with heart-melting softness in his eyes, even if he had just called me an idiot. "This wasn't about you coming here for your happiness, this was about you coming here for everyone else's happiness. Look around and tell me the common thing that's linking everyone's smiles?"

I scanned the room, from Gran adoringly fussing over Amber who was nestled in her pleased as punch father's arms, onto John who had said something that had Ashley crying with laughter whilst Lucy swatted him in the stomach, then to the man who was looking at me as if I was the only person in the world.

"It's you," he answered for me. "You're the catalyst for all for this. If you hadn't caused all that hassle in my restaurant that day, Lucy and Ashley probably wouldn't have had a reason to speak to each other, which means John and Ryan wouldn't have formed their friendship either and none of them would have benefitted from your grandmother's cooking or wisdom. Then there's me."

"And what was it I did for you?" I asked, trying to sound playful but my windpipe was clogged with all kinds of emotion.

"You were my own personal sunshine. You made me happy again, shining through those dark clouds with your bloody persistent need to be liked by everyone, eventually getting to me. You made me risk opening myself up again and I've never been happier."

My eyes immediately started to sting as I forced myself not to cry because if any prospective customers happened to walk in and saw me in floods of tears, they'd probably walk straight backout again.

"Rob! Stop upsetting Jess before we've even opened," Lucy cried as she walked over to us and grabbed my hand. "Come on, we're almost ready. Everyone, gather round!"

Our small group followed Lucy's orders as John appeared from behind a dressing screen with a tray of wine glasses and began handing them out.

"Right. Before we do this, we need an opening speech to christen the shop. Come on Jess."

My eyes widened as I looked at Lucy. "Why me?"

"Because none of this would have happened without you," she said, rolling her eyes as if it were obvious.

Everyone else then began tapping their glasses and shouting for a speech, so I was left with no choice.

"Ok, ok. I'm going to keep this short and sweet." I then thought about what Rob had said to me about all of this happening because I was here but I still couldn't agree with him. "I'll start by saying that Lucy is wrong. This hasn't all happened because of me. This has happened because of all of us and for all the hard work we've put into it. This has happened because I dated a tosser whose actions led me here to escape and find a new life. This has happened because a guy who was bad at his job allowed me to make two of the greatest friends anyone could ask for. This has happened because of Gran and her love of sewing. This happened because I thought being part of a sewing bee would be good for me. This happened because Lucy had a dream. This happened because three strong, smart women refused to let life get them down and take no for an answer. This happened because these same three women were strong enough and smart enough to make the men in their lives help build this without having to pay them."

I paused as John raised his glass and shouted out. The break also gave me a second to breathe and regain my control as I was very nearly on the verge of happy tears. Again.

"What I'm trying to say is that all of this was possible because of every, single person in this room. It looks amazing and we can all be so proud of what we have built. So, if you would raise your glasses, I would firstly like to propose a toast to the original Sewing Sisters and the honorary members. And my second toast is to love and friendship. Without it, none of us would be here today."

The room echoed my toast before everyone began clapping and I exhaled my sigh of relief.

As if from far away, I then heard Ashley's voice rallying everyone into position as it was almost time, but someone had already pulled me in for a tight hug. I instinctively knew it was Rob.

"I love you," he whispered in my ear.

I pulled back and smiled at him but didn't get the chance to reply.

"Ready?" Lucy shouted from the door, her face aglow with the anticipation we were all feeling, her hand resting on the door handle.

The Universe certainly worked in weird ways, but I had the feeling that all roads were supposed to lead here, and I was finally exactly where I was meant to be.

"Ladies and gentlemen, Deja Vintage is officially open for business."

Also available by Megan Musgrove

Taming Her Stallion

(Self-Made Rouge Series – Book 1)

England, 1817 - Lady Felicity Greene is perfectly content living the quiet life on her family's Suffolk estate, but when two men turn up claiming to be interested in purchasing a racehorse from her father, the peace is broken. It doesn't matter how handsome one of the men is, there is clearly something foul afoot, and Felicity is intent on finding out what is it.

Jack Rockall would do anything for his friend and business partner Ian, including agreeing to accompany him to the Marquess of Sharnbrook's estate and entertaining his spinster daughter, while Ian can investigate a family secret that has plagued him all his life. Only, distracting the Lady Felicity proves to be a task and a half the second Jack lays eyes on her.

Baby, It's Cold Outside

Beth Michaels tries to avoid two things – men and Christmas. But when a shock redundancy sends her to the countryside to reassess her life, she gets an unhealthy dose of both. Will her attractive new neighbour Aidan find a way to breech the walls Beth has set up around herself or will the self-confessed workaholic find an excuse to run back to the city to spend another Christmas morning alone?

Bent Out of Shape

A chance encounter on an aeroplane throws a man Lily
had never expected to see again, back into her life.

Yoga instructor Lily Stewart fights her attraction to
workaholic commitaphobe Dylan, the boy she grew up
with. Aside from the fact he tormented her when they
were children, he "doesn't do love". Starting
something up with him would just get messy, and Lily
is all about clean living.

The Art of Love

Ally Spencer has a lot going for her. She has a great job, a great flat, and great friends. But after her little sister's wedding announcement is made, old memories of her fiancé, who broke things off only a few months before, begin resurfacing. Feeling the need for a night on the town, she overdoes it slightly and finds herself in a handsome stranger's hotel room the following morning with no memory of how she ended up there. After bolting, she tries to put the experience behind her only to find this mysterious man popping up in her personal and professional life. Along with fighting a growing attraction for a man she is sure she should dislike, she is roped into helping with her perfect sister's OTT wedding plans.

Viva Las Vegas

Ally and Tom decide to take that trip to Las Vegas, with Chris and Sara in tow. But in a city where normal life does not exist, will the four of them recover from the tests Sin City throws at them?

Does what happens in Vegas really stay in Vegas?

Printed by Amazon Italia Logistica S.r.l.
Torrazza Piemonte (TO), Italy